What if...

All Your Friends Turned on You

Catch up on all the

What if . . . books!

What if . . . Everyone Knew Your Name

What if . . . All the Boys Wanted You

What if . . . You Broke All the Rules

What if . . . Everyone Was Doing It

What if . . . All the Rumors Were True

What if . . . Your Past Came Back to Haunt You

What if . . . All Your Friends Turned On You

And coming in December 2009:

What if . . . All Your Dreams Came True

a choose your destiny NOVEL

What if...

All Your Friends Turned On You

LIZ RUCKDESCHEL AND SARA JAMES

DELACORTE PRESS

 Published by Delacorte Press, an imprint of Random House Children's Books, a division of Random House, Inc., New York.

Delacorte Press is a registered trademark and the colophon is a trademark of Random House, Inc.

Visit us on the Web! www.randomhouse.com/teens

Educators and librarians, for a variety of teaching tools, visit us at www.randomhouse.com/teachers

Library of Congress Cataloging-in Publication Data is available upon request.
ISBN 978-0-385-73818-7 (tr. pbk.)—
ISBN 978-0-375-89339-1 (e-book)

The text of this book is set in 12.5-point Apollo.

Book design by Marci Senders

Printed in the United States of America

10 9 8 7 6 5 4 3 2 1

ARMCHAIR LIBERALS

Sometimes "auld acquaintance" should be forgot.

"More mock-n-cheese, honey?"

Haley Miller watched as Mrs. Armstrong plopped a mound of macaroni and tofu concoction onto her husband's plate. Dinner had ended for everyone else, but Doug Armstrong clearly couldn't get enough of this gelatinous stuff. And apparently, neither could Annie Armstrong's boyfriend, Dave Metzger.

"I'll take some more too, please, Mrs. Armstrong," Dave said, holding out his plate. "There's nothing like a big helping of mock-n-cheese. Mock cheese tastes better than real cheese any day, I think."

"I totally agree," Mr. Armstrong said. Dave beamed at him. And Annie smiled at the two of them, obviously pleased to see them getting along so well.

Haley shifted uncomfortably in her seat. It was weird to see just how alike Annie's father and her boyfriend were. They both had wiry, frizzy hair and bad skin. Even their names—Doug and Dave—were quite similar. The thought that Annie might like Dave because he was so much like her dad made Haley suddenly queasy—though the rumbling in her tumbling could have been the mock-n-cheese. It was probably both.

"It's almost time for the ball to drop," Haley said. Any excuse to get away from the faux gras. "Shouldn't we move into the living room and turn on the TV?"

"The city of New York wastes so much energy lighting up that silly ball," Haley's mother, Joan Miller, said. "I don't know whether to feel guilty for watching it and therefore supporting it, or guilty for depriving my kids of the communal experience."

"I know what you mean, Joan," Blythe Armstrong said. "But if they're going to use the energy, we might as well enjoy it."

The entire group stood up and waddled, full of

vegetables and tofu, into the living room. It was New Year's Eve, and the Miller family—Haley, her seven-year-old brother, Mitchell, and their parents, Joan and Perry—were celebrating quietly with Annie Armstrong's family and a few friends. Annie's mother, Blythe, was an environmental lawyer at Armstrong & White, the firm where Joan worked, so the conversation was never lacking on the granola front.

Blythe Armstrong poured champagne for Haley's parents and sparkling apple cider for the minors while Annie turned on the TV. It wasn't the most exciting New Year's Eve Haley could imagine—far from it—but she tried to make the best of it. At least she had some friends with her, even if they were mostly of the brainiac variety: Annie, Dave, their classmate Hannah Moss and star debater and politico Alex Martin, who cochaired the debate team with Annie. Alex stood out, even in this supersmart and super-ambitious crowd, but it was mostly for his conservative political views. He worked as an intern for New Jersey's Republican governor-elect, Eleanor Eton, known in the Miller household as Public Enemy Number One.

Haley didn't agree with Alex's politics, but she found him the most interesting person at the party to talk to. And, in his bookish way, he was also the cutest.

"Maybe they should light the ball with nuclear

power," Doug Armstrong said. "That would save a lot of energy, uh-heh, uh-heh." That odd pseudo-laugh he tacked onto the end of his sentence struck Haley as strangely familiar. She didn't have to wait long to figure out why.

"Sure—and possibly blow the city to smithereens," Dave said. "That'd be cool, uh-heh, uh-heh."

"Nuclear power? Not that again," Perry said. "I did a doc on no-nukes fifteen years ago. I thought we'd settled the whole nuclear thing, and if Washington hadn't been too mired in lobbyist politics to push forward on greener technology, it would have stayed settled."

Haley's father, Perry, was a documentary filmmaker who taught at Columbia and shared a liberal activist bent with his wife. Haley was all for liberal activism too; she just didn't find it scintillating party chat. She slid a silver elastic off her wrist and pulled her shoulder-length auburn hair into a loose ponytail. Why even bother looking glam for this crowd? Might as well get comfortable, since it looked as if she was in for a long night of discussing the pros and cons of clean energy sources.

"Nuclear power is a lot safer than it used to be," Alex protested. "And it's way cleaner than oil."

"Nuclear power will never be safe enough for me," Perry said. "What do we do with the waste?"

"What do you suggest we use instead, Perry?" Blythe said. "So-called clean coal?"

"I think clean coal's not a bad way to go, actually," Doug chimed in.

"There's no such thing," Joan said. "It's an oxymoron, like healthy cigarettes. Al Gore is right about that, at least."

"You should see what coal mining does to the Appalachians, too," Perry said. "It's like an open wound on the land, and the people who live there deal with all kinds of contamination. . . ."

"Well, we've got to use something to fuel our economy," Doug said. "I don't suppose anybody here is in favor of offshore drilling for more oil."

"No!" Perry, Joan and Blythe shouted at once.

"Uh, it's New Year's Eve," Haley said. "Do you think we could talk about something a little more . . . festive?"

"Like what?" Annie said.

"How about Mrs. Eton's upcoming inauguration?" Alex suggested.

Joan Miller looked horrified. "Look, Alex, you're a nice boy—a little misguided, maybe, but nice. What are you trying to do here, start a fistfight?"

"There's no issue more compelling to me right now than the environment," Blythe said. "I'd say this is our World War Three."

"I'll settle this," Haley said. "The obvious compromise is a blend of traditional and alternative energy sources. End of discussion. See how easy that was?"

"My practical daughter," Joan said. "We forgot about solar."

Doug scoffed. "Please. Next you'll be telling me to convert my diesel car to vegetable oil."

"That really works, you know, Dad," Annie said.

"Haley will be getting her driver's license soon," Perry said. "Only a month and a half from now. I have to admit that thought scares me a little."

Haley was offended. "I'll be a good driver, Dad."

"I'm sure you will," Perry said. "It just gives us another thing to worry about: car accidents."

"Will you be getting a car for your birthday, Haley?" Alex asked.

"I don't know," Haley replied, nodding toward her parents. "Ask them."

"She might be," Joan said with a knowing smirk.

"There may be a little surprise in the driveway come February fourteenth," Perry added, a little too confidently.

"Really?" Haley smiled. A lot of her friends had gotten cars for their seventeenth birthdays, but she hadn't expected her own parents to buy one for her. As far as Joan and Perry were concerned, mass transit was always the best way to travel, and Haley could take the bus. Or so she thought anyway. The idea that they might be softening in their old age and that she might actually get a car of her very own was the most exciting news she'd heard all night. In fact, it almost made up for the mock-n-cheese.

"We'll see," Joan added, noticing the look of glee on Haley's face and tempering her enthusiasm. "Let's not get our hopes up."

"My electric car is very reliable, Mr. and Mrs. Miller," Annie said, dropping a not-so-subtle hint.

"Sure—as long as you plug it in every two hours," Doug countered. "And where do you think the electricity comes from—Santa Claus?"

"Speaking of, did you see the Santa they had at the mall this year?" Dave interjected. "He had a really great . . . lap."

"Excuse me?" Haley turned to gape at him. Dave had been off his game lately—that is to say, even weirder than usual—but this was an odd comment even for the Metzger.

Dave had been raised by a single mom—Nora—but the previous fall he had tracked down and contacted his long-lost biological father, hoping for a reunion. Instead, his father refused to see him. The whole experience had been, well, rough on Dave, and he was clearly not over it. Not that Dave was ever what you'd call normal, but now, in addition to being neurotic, he was positively erratic at times. And to make matters worse, Dave's mother had recently gotten much more serious with her boyfriend, Rick Von, director of the art program at Hillsdale High—in other words, one of Dave's teachers. Let's just say Dave wasn't taking it all in stride.

"The Santa at the mall?" Haley said. "You actually sat? On his lap?"

"Didn't you? He had a quality, don't you think?" Dave replied. "I think I'll try to book him on the podcast. He's got just the kind of lap that makes you want to tell him all your secrets. Or something. Uh-heh, uh-heh."

Dave had always been obsessed with his Internet video broadcast, "Inside Hillsdale," but now he'd begun planning a special variety-show holiday edition called "Our Spectacular, Spectacular Hillsdale." For it, he'd lined up a juggler, a barbershop quartet and a contortionist, but he was always on the lookout for new talent—if you could call it that.

"Can I be on the show?" Haley's little brother, Mitchell, asked. "I could be your sidekick, like Ed McMahon."

Mitchell was a bit of an obsessive oddball himself, his latest craze being vintage TV talk shows. Tonight, for instance, he was dressed for the party in a bright red blazer and a gaudy patterned tie, just like a pocket-sized Lawrence Welk. It had become his signature of late. If he was going to a casual event—say, like school—he ditched the blazer and went with more of a golf-pro-style pastel polo shirt and khakis, but otherwise, the synthetic tie-jacket combo was in full effect. It was certainly a strange look for a second grader, but then, Haley had sort of gotten used to it, and at least Mitchell was no longer communicating in his stiff robotic voice. Now, that was a phase Haley was glad her brother had outgrown.

"Interesting," Dave said, considering Mitchell's proposition. "What sort of experience do you have?"

"Oh, I host my own variety show," Mitchell said matter-of-factly. "In our living room. I'm really good, aren't I, Haley?"

"His light comedy puts your barbershop quartet to shame," Haley noted.

"Hmm." Dave stroked his pimply chin while across the room, Haley couldn't help but notice, Doug Armstrong rubbed the stubble on his chin in almost the exact same fashion. The symmetry of their movements made Haley shiver. "A dwarf cohost could be kind of entertaining. . . ."

"I'm not a dwarf," Mitchell countered.

"Right, right," Dave said. "Let me think about it, Mitchie. I'll get back to you. Or better yet, have your people call mine."

"But I don't have any people." Mitchell frowned. "Mom, where can I get some people?"

"Maybe you could have RoBro! host the show," Annie suggested.

"RoBro!'s not even close to being ready yet," Hannah said.

Alex looked confused, and then he asked the question Haley was afraid he was about to utter. "What's RoBro!?"

Oh no, Haley thought, *here we go.*

"RoBro! is a robot brother," Dave said. "Or sister. I'm sure he could be adjusted to be a girl, if that was what you wanted."

"He's perfect for the only child," Hannah said. "Like me, or Dave. Or Annie, come to think of it."

"It's my creation. The idea was born out of loneliness," Dave said.

"I never wanted a sibling," Annie said, flashing her parents a look of gratitude.

"I had a RoBro! of my own until a few months ago," Haley said, giving Mitchell an affectionate pinch.

"I don't know about RoBro!s, but just plain old brothers are pretty great," Alex said. He had two of them himself, both younger.

"We're planning to unveil RoBro! next fall," Dave said. "At our MIT interviews."

"RoBro! will ro-blow their minds," Hannah said. "We're shoo-ins."

"I don't think anyone is a shoo-in at MIT these days, my dear," Doug Armstrong said, clearly pleased with himself and his alma mater. "Unless, of course, you're a legacy." He eyed Annie.

What a buzzkill, Haley thought. Boy, was he in for a surprise. Annie wasn't even intending to apply to MIT and had set her sights on Yale.

Haley, Dave, Annie and Hannah were only juniors,

but at least three of them were already totally obsessed with getting into the right university next year. Alex, meanwhile, was currently a senior. His applications had been completed and submitted weeks ago. Haley had gathered that his first choice was Georgetown, where he hoped to major in political science. With his wholesome good looks, preppy attire and formidable IQ, Haley figured he'd fit right in.

Hannah and Dave, on the other hand, were so socially awkward, they were both probably a long shot for their first choice, MIT, unless someone gave them some immediate charm lessons.

"Why do I get the feeling RoBro! will be obsolete before he's had a chance to launch his first spitball?" Haley whispered to Alex.

"I always thought of RoBro! as more of a paper airplane kind of guy," he whispered back.

Even though Haley and Alex were the political equivalent of oil and water, she couldn't help but feel drawn to him. Then again, Haley felt drawn to a lot of people, including her hot neighbor, Reese Highland, and the cute and almost painfully withdrawn photographer in her class, Devon McKnight. In the back of her mind, Haley had been hoping to spend a little New Year's quality time with Reese, but she hadn't heard from him in weeks and was left wondering whether he even remembered her phone number.

Not that he needed to—he lived right next door, after all. So where on earth had he been hiding?

Alex wasn't at all like Reese, that was for sure. And okay, he could be infuriating sometimes, like whenever he tried to explain trickle-down economics. But she had the feeling that if she said the word, Alex would be there for her. Could the same be said for Reese? She was almost positive the answer would be an emphatic *no* when it came to Devon's reliability.

"You guys want to come over and see the 'Bro!?" Dave said. "He's in my garage—well, Mr. Von's garage." He swallowed painfully but mustered the courage to go on. "We've got a lot of kinks to work out, but you can get a feel for how wonderful the android family of the future will be."

Haley hesitated. She'd had more than enough of the Armstrongs' nutritionally and environmentally correct hospitality—it felt a little too much like home at times—but ending the evening with the robot family of the future was not exactly a glamorous alternative. She was about to nudge her parents and plead for an early night when her cell phone buzzed. "Incoming," she said, opening it up to read the text. Suddenly she had three messages waiting for her. Maybe the night would be saved after all.

Haley tucked into a corner of the couch for privacy and saw that the texts were coming so fast and furiously, she couldn't even tell who they were from.

Not that it mattered—it was the attached pictures that delivered the punch to her stomach.

"Chk the boyz in nevis!" the message blared, accompanied by a photo of a handsome sun-kissed guy clearly enjoying himself on a Caribbean beach with a bikini-clad babe on his lap.

"Oh my God," Haley gasped. It was none other than Spencer Eton, the rich bad boy of Hillsdale High, son of soon-to-be-governor Eleanor Eton and boyfriend of class queen bee Coco De Clerq. Haley had gotten to know Coco fairly well in the year and a half since she'd moved to New Jersey from California—well enough to know a picture like this was bound to send Coco into a murderous rampage.

But that wasn't the end of it. The first picture was followed by one horrifying photo after another. There was rocker Johnny Lane, looking more Beach Boy than Mr. Clash, doing the twist with a redheaded beauty who was definitely *not* his girlfriend, Sasha Lewis. There was superjock Drew Napolitano with a neon blue umbrella drink in one hand and a copper-skinned model's waist in the other—an image sure to crush the heart of his cheerleader girlfriend, Cecily Watson. In fact, all of these boys had girlfriends back at home in Hillsdale—pretty, loyal, loving girlfriends who at this very moment were sure to be looking at the barrage of snapshots, just as Haley was.

She opened another text, and there was Spencer again, this time with a leggy strawberry blonde riding piggyback and clinging to his shoulders, her legs wrapped around his waist. Haley thought she could hear Coco's screams all the way from the De Clerqs' McMansion in the Heights, and resolved to text Coco some sympathetic words of support as soon as the parade of texts stopped polluting her cell phone.

And then— *Oh no.* It couldn't be. Haley had to look away for a second. She looked back. It was!

There was Reese Highland, his black hair being mussed by a buxom brunette, flashing his perfect white teeth in a wide, charming grin.

Not Reese! How could this be? Drinking was so not Reese's style. In fact, he was so straight-edge his friends called him Natural Highland as a joke.

Haley swallowed hard, her stomach in knots. "No wonder I haven't heard from him all week," she muttered to herself.

She closed her eyes, but the image was now seared in her brain: virtuous Reese partying with the bad boys and fraternizing with a fleshbot who was clearly no RoBro!

Of course Haley had heard about Spencer's plans for a trip to Nevis, organized by his mother. The governor-elect had very prudently decided to send her hard-partying son and his friends far from prying eyes, to an island in the Caribbean purposely chosen for its peace, quiet, serenity and lack of nightlife. The last thing she needed was another Spencer-related scandal to divert attention from her upcoming inauguration—and if left to his own devices in town, with two weeks off from school and nothing but time on his hands, Spencer was sure to get up to something.

What Mrs. Eton hadn't counted on, apparently, was a hot calendar photo shoot taking place at the boys' peaceful, quiet hotel. And what Haley hadn't counted on was Reese joining the party. Of course Reese played sports and was friendly with Spencer, Drew and Johnny, but in the year that she had known him he'd never been a partier. In fact, he'd been so tense about college lately that he spent all his free time studying.

Or so he'd always told Haley. But now, who knew what he'd been up to all those times he'd said he was at the library?

Haley clicked off her phone, wishing the terrible images would just go away. Had Reese changed? Or had she never really known him? This kind of shock was definitely not on her holiday wish list. All she could think about was finding the fastest way to the Returns Department. Or at the very least, Complaints.

"Is everything okay, Haley?" Alex asked. Behind him, on the TV, the countdown was beginning: ten, nine, eight . . .

"Um, not really," Haley said.

And then Mitchell screamed, "Happy New Year!" and the room erupted around her.

● ● ●

Haley had better hope the old maxim about New Year's Eve isn't true—that the way you spend that night is the way you'll spend the rest of the year. If that's the case, her year is going to be filled with stomachaches, heartaches and something called a RoBro! Not a happy prospect.

Those beach bunny shots are pretty shocking—and all the other spurned girls at Hillsdale High are sure to be as irked as Haley is. Hell hath no fury like a Coquette scorned, and sometimes a little fury is just what a girl needs to get a bad boy out of her system.

If you think Haley's top priority is to get to the bottom of those pix and get some moral support from her fellow victims, have her band together with her lady friends in NEW YEAR, NEW YOU on page 33.

Maybe you think some decent food is in order after all that mock-n-cheese and faux gras. If so, head to the Golden Dynasty in WET NOODLE on page 18.

On the other hand, even perennial parent-pleasers Annie and Dave seemed bored at the Armstrongs' bash tonight. If you think the quickest and easiest way for Haley to forget her troubles is to duck out of the party and go meet the future in the form of Dave's animated automaton, turn to page 26, SMALL WONDER.

Haley did get one good shock tonight: the news that her parents are considering giving her a car for her seventeenth birthday. So things aren't looking all bad for the new year. Then again, why was Haley ringing it in at a lame party with her parents? Didn't any more appealing invitations come her way?

Now that Hillsdale's heartthrobs have all turned on their girls, who will be the next victim of a disloyal act? With the boys in Nevis, where did Coco and her friends ring in the new year? And what about the arty crowd, Irene, Shaun and Devon? Did everyone make plans behind Haley's back?

When your friends all turn on you, life can get lonely fast. Maybe Haley should stick close to those she knows best. Or at least buy herself a RoBro!

WET NOODLE

At most Chinese restaurants, canoodling is not on the menu.

"What's with the outfit?" Haley asked. "Did your dad declare an end to the dress code or something?"

Haley's classmate Irene Chen was greeting customers at the hostess station of her parents' restaurant, the Golden Dynasty, in a sexy-punk outfit—a ripped T-shirt, plaid miniskirt and combat boots. This was typical of her uniform for school, but for work, Irene's father expected her to wear hostess whites—a crisp button-down shirt tucked into a long demure skirt. He had recently invested in the getup to class up the joint.

"This is how I always dress," Irene said defiantly. "Why should I change to please someone else? He's not the boss of me."

"Actually," Haley said, "he is. If you want to get technical about it." She was pretty sure Irene didn't.

"Well, he acts more like a dictator, if you ask me," Irene said. "Especially ever since he caught me and Shaun in the basement."

"Caught you and Shaun . . . doing what, exactly?" Haley wasn't sure she wanted to know.

"What do you think?" Irene said. "Hooking up, snogging, rounding home plate—whatever you want to call it. Dad didn't like it. He said that from now on I have to go straight to work after school and straight home after work, nowhere else. I'm basically grounded for life. Or I would be if I listened to his Stalinesque rules."

Irene and her boyfriend, Shaun Willkommen, were one of Hillsdale's longest-running couples. Shaun was blond and potbellied and strange, but so deeply himself it gave him a certain irresistible charm. They were among the most talented artists in school and very rebellious, though Irene had been restricting most of her rebellion to outside the home—until recently, that is. Shaun was more of a free spirit, letting the wind take him wherever it blew, which for Shaun was often in truly bizarre directions.

"Whatever," Irene said. "What's wrong with you? Your skin looks kind of . . . greenish."

"I think it's my mother's cooking," Haley said. "Two weeks of nothing but veggies is literally turning me green." Not to mention the disturbing pictures that had just flooded her cell phone of Hillsdale's finest cavorting with swimsuit models. That was enough to make anyone sick. "I need some double-deep-fried sesame chicken, extra spicy, and I need it now."

"I'll put in an order for you, but I've got to warn you, don't look around or you might lose your appetite." Irene scribbled down the order and took it to the kitchen.

Haley couldn't resist scanning the restaurant after a warning like that, but she soon regretted it. The Dynasty was open late for the holiday, and hopping. Nothing unappetizing about that. It was what Haley spotted by the koi pond that sent her stomach lurching.

There, in a cozy corner booth, were Devon McKnight and his freshman sidekick, Darcy Podowski. Devon's ever-present camera sat on the table beside them while he and his platinum blond neighbor from the Floods snuggled up together, whispering and laughing in each other's ears. Devon closed his eyes as pale, skinny Darcy ran her fingers through his sandy brown hair.

Haley wanted to turn away from this crime scene, but she couldn't. *They must be hooking up by now,* she thought in despair. But then again, with Devon, who knew. It wasn't as if he were very adept at expressing himself or making the first—make that second, third, fourth or even fifth—move.

Haley had always thought Devon was adorable in an artsy-misfit way, and for a while, he seemed to like her too. Then little Darcy showed up and started distracting Devon from his aimless pursuit of Haley. Okay, so he was quite easily distracted. Whenever he started to really dig a girl, his self-destructive tendencies kicked in and made him pull away. So why wasn't he hightailing it out of the restaurant right now? Devon hadn't pulled away from Darcy. Not yet, anyway.

Haley tried to console herself by thinking of sesame chicken, but it wasn't working. Devon looked up and caught her eye. She didn't look away, and neither did he. His sexy gaze had always been able to keep her spellbound. At least when he turned it her way.

If only he weren't such a project, Haley thought. She wondered what it would take to get him to make an actual decision about dating a girl, instead of just making out with whoever was in his orbit that week.

Darcy finally noticed she'd lost Devon's attention for the moment and looked up to see what was catching his eye. When she saw it was Haley, her expression changed from moony to mean. She tossed Haley a quick stink-eye and turned Devon's face back toward her.

Might as well check on my food, Haley thought, resigned to leave Devon to his wishy-washy ways. She turned to the register to see Mr. Chen sputtering with rage at Irene. "I told you not to leave the house like that and how do I find you? In a harlot skirt and Hell Angel boots! Not decent! Go home and change into your uniform! I won't have you in my restaurant dressed like this!"

"You can't tell me what to do!" Irene barked back. Heads from the nearby tables began to turn toward the hostess station to see what the commotion was about. "I'm an adult!"

"You are seventeen! Still child!" Mr. Chen shouted.

"Okay, I'm nearly an adult," Irene said. "And you'd better get used to the idea. I'm not backing down this time, Pops—not about my clothes, and not about Shaun."

"Shaun! That boy is a dragon! I forbid you to see him ever again!" Mr. Chen's face was turning purple.

"You can scream all you want," Irene said, reining in her anger. "I don't care what you say. I'm seventeen years old. I will wear whatever I want, and I will do whatever I want to with my boyfriend. And you can't stop me." She grabbed Haley by the arm and pulled her toward the door. "See ya later, Pops. I quit!"

"Come back here!" Mr. Chen yelled. "You can't walk out on me! We're shorthanded tonight! Get back here! Irene!"

By now the whole restaurant was watching. Irene dragged Haley outside to the parking lot, where they shivered in the frosty January night as Irene lit a cigarette. She had only recently taken up smoking, and Haley could tell she didn't enjoy it. Not one little bit.

"What are we going to do now?" Haley asked as Irene tried to cover up a cough. "Maybe you should go back and apologize."

"Are you crazy?" Irene said. "I totally did the right thing. I can't let him run my life. He'd keep me locked in my room forever if he could. It's still early. Let's go somewhere."

"Okay, but what about my sesame chicken?"

Irene nearly snarled at her. "You know, you'd be a lot better off if you spent less time thinking of ways to stuff your face and more time trying to wrench Devon free from that devil-cat Darcy."

"Even if I did take on the Devon Project, I'd still need to eat," Haley said sulkily.

"Come on, Shaun's parents are having a New Year's Eve party," Irene said. "Let's crash it. I'm sure there'll be food there."

"What kind of food?" Haley asked petulantly.

"Something good," Irene said. "They're the Willkommens. Now let's go, Haley, I'm freezing. Quick, before my dad comes out and tries to chain me to the hostess station."

As they started walking up the hill toward Shaun's house, Irene turned to Haley and asked, "Did you hear the news about Rick Von Wrinkle? Engaged."

"Whoa, no way. To Dave Metzger's mother?" Haley asked. She knew that Mr. Von and Mrs. Metzger had been dating for a while, but the news still took her by surprise, especially since Dave hadn't mentioned it at the Armstrongs' house. She wondered if he even knew.

"There's an engagement party next week. We're all invited."

"Is Devon going?" Haley asked.

"Highly unlikely," Irene said. "Darcy wasn't included, and he doesn't go anywhere these days without Tattoo Barbie. But that doesn't mean I'm letting you off the hook." Irene paused. "For what it's worth, I still think you could snag him for good with a little effort, and then we could give Darcy the boot."

Haley thought it over for a minute. Was Irene right about Devon? Should Haley be trying to pull him out of Darcy's vampy clutches before it was too late? Or should she trust her first instinct, forget him and move on?

• • •

Devon's always been confusing, and frankly, his push/pull act with Haley has gotten old. But what if Irene is right? It's not as if Haley's been trying very hard to win him over. Maybe the Devon chapter in Haley's life isn't over yet. What if all she needs is one last effort to lure him away?

If you think Irene has a point and Haley should fight for Devon's affections before she writes him off, go to page 47, TRIPLE DATE.

But then, look at all the advantages Darcy has. She's got the arty rebel thing down, which is a proven winner with Devon. She seems to have nothing but time on her hands to spend trying to please him. And she lives next door to the guy, for heaven's sake. Haley knows from her experience with Reese that sometimes nothing beats proximity. Maybe Haley should just give up. Why waste her time on a lost cause?

If you think Haley should leave Devon alone to be devoured by Darcy, head off with Irene to their art teacher's engagement party on page 59, VON-METZGER. Who knows, maybe she'll find someone interesting there.

SMALL WONDER

Do robots feel pain?

"The days of being an only child are over," Dave Metzger announced. He was in Mr. Von's garage, surrounded by Haley, Alex, Annie and Hannah, waving his arm over a three-foot-tall pile of something with a sheet over it. "I give you—RoBro!"

He whipped the sheet off the small figure. There in front of them was a metal creature on wheels, with metal arms dangling lifelessly at its sides. A sweater had been pulled over the top half of the "torso," which was crowned by a large, rubbery doll's head.

Dave must have had trouble finding a boy doll big enough to work with, because he'd taken a girl doll's head and given it a boy's haircut. It was the creepiest thing Haley had ever seen.

"Ta-da!" Hannah said.

"I think Dave's abandonment issues have gotten way out of hand," Alex murmured to Haley.

"You couldn't pay me to live in the same house with that thing," Haley whispered back.

"Let's see it do something," Annie said.

"All right," Dave said. "Remember, he's a work in progress. We've still got a long way to go. Hannah, would you do the honors?"

"Uh, well, the 'Bro! doesn't really do all that much yet," Hannah said. "I can try to make him wave, but I've got to hard-wire the circuitry before it will work."

She started fiddling with some wires at the back of the RoBro! Anyone else would have had to stoop down to reach the wires, but Hannah was so small she barely had to bend her knees. To pass the time, Haley flipped through some of Mr. Von's old vinyl records, looking for something festive to play among all the classic jazz and folk. Alex grabbed a Miles Davis record and put it on the old turntable.

"So, um, I guess the RoBro! won't be the only new addition to my family," Dave said as the music filled the dimly lit garage.

"What do you mean?" Haley asked. "Your

mother's not pregnant, is she? Because I don't know if it's the best idea for Mr. Von to breed."

"Ha! Wouldn't that be fitting?" Annie said. "If Mrs. Metzger had a baby just when Dave is building a robot brother?"

"No, she's not having a baby . . . that I know of," Dave said. Haley was struck by the rattled look on his face and felt sorry for him. "She's—she's getting married. To Mr. Von, of course."

This announcement was met with stunned silence, except for the scratchy trumpet music playing through the speakers. Haley didn't know what to say. Nora Metzger was already living with Mr. Von, so it really wouldn't make much difference in Dave's life. But knowing the situation was permanent might not be easy for him to take.

Annie threw her arms around Dave's neck and said, "Isn't it wonderful? I love weddings."

"When did this happen?" Haley asked.

"Over Christmas," Dave said, cracking a tight smile. "Annie's right, it really is great. I couldn't be happier for them. They're having an engagement party Saturday night—and I want you all to come. We'll all celebrate together."

"Where's the party?" Alex asked.

"Here, at Mr. Von's house," Dave said.

"You mean, here at your new house," Hannah said. "You better start getting comfortable here. It's not temporary anymore."

"No, I guess you're right . . . ," Dave said, his face going white.

"Is Mr. Von going to adopt you?" Alex asked. Haley slid her hand across her throat in a "Cut! Cut!" gesture, but it was too late. "Will you change your name to Dave Von? Or maybe Dave Von-Metzger? That sounds pretty impressive."

The blood drained from Dave's face until he was ghostly pale. Annie, looking horrified, stepped behind him and held out her arms, ready to catch her boyfriend if he fainted.

"Not cool," Annie said to Alex. "Really not cool."

"What's wrong with hyphenating?" Alex asked, aghast.

"I will never take that man's name as long as I live," Dave declared.

"There's no reason to," Haley assured him. "I'm sure it's fine if you stick with just plain old Metzger." She wished he'd just sit down already and let the blood flow back to his face. Sheet-white was not a good look for Dave.

Annie tried to change the subject. "How's that wiring coming, Hannah?"

"I think I can make him talk," Hannah said. "Once we got him to say 'How are you.'"

She straightened up and flicked a switch on the robot's back. RoBro! made a whirring sound and turned his head slightly. His mouth didn't move but a faint sound did come out of the little speaker in his chest. Annie put her ear to the speaker.

"What's he saying?" Haley asked.

"It sounds like 'Ow ow ow,'" Annie said.

"He's still loaded with bugs," Dave conceded. "Maybe we'll be able to demonstrate a few of the things he can do at the big engagement party."

"Yeah, about that. I'd like to come," Alex said. "I really would. And I promise to try, but I'm not sure I can make it. Governor Eton's inauguration is coming up, and I'm helping to organize the inaugural ball. It's insanely complicated, coordinating all the food and flowers and caterers and stuff, and everything always seems to be an emergency. It's taking up all my time. I doubt I'll have a social life until it's over, unfortunately. But we'll see."

Alex was an intern in Eleanor Eton's office, and he was so capable he'd been given as much responsibility as some of her aides.

"I can't believe you're celebrating that woman's inauguration," Annie said. "She'll set the state back fifty years."

"But I bet it's going to be a fabulous party," Hannah offered.

"You're telling me," Alex said. "Eleanor Eton does not have simple tastes."

No, she definitely does not, Haley thought. She couldn't help wondering what the ball would be like. It was sure to be lavish, but in what way? What did

Alex's duties entail, exactly? And who would be invited?

More importantly, would Alex be allowed to bring a date? What if a certain someone, say, Haley, helped him prepare for the big event—would that certain someone be allowed to attend?

There was a lot to think about. And a lot of groundwork to be laid.

• • •

So, Dave's mom is marrying the wacky Mr. Von. It's not as if anyone couldn't see it coming—anyone but Dave, that is. Most of the kids at Hillsdale like Mr. Von. However, having him as a stepfather is another story.

Still, the big Von-Metzger engagement party is sure to be an unmissable event, with lots of Mr. Von's favorite students—meaning the art crowd—in attendance. If you're positive that Haley would never skip this milestone in Hillsdale student history, turn to page 59, VON-METZGER.

On the other hand, Eleanor Eton's inauguration is a milestone of another sort, and her outrageous ball is likely to draw a totally different crowd: the social princes and princesses not only of Hillsdale but the whole state of New Jersey. With Alex spending all his free time preparing for it, what should Haley do? Alex already said he'd have no social life until after the ball. But then, there are always ways around that. Haley could socialize with him by working at Mrs. Eton's

headquarters, helping him get ready for the big day. So what if her family disowned her.

If you think Haley would rather see state politics—and Alex—up close rather than make small talk at a teacher's house, turn to page 69, POLITICAL PREP.

You can think big, or you can think small. Of course, the higher you reach, the farther you can fall.

NEW YEAR, NEW YOU

New Year's resolutions are meant to be broken.

"Haley, glad you're here." Coco barked at her like a general. "Close the door and sit down. We've got work to do."

It was New Year's Eve—still a holiday, last Haley checked—and Coco's large bedroom suite was decked out for a party. There were platters of food and bottles of bubbly, and the guests—Sasha Lewis, Whitney Klein and Cecily Watson, all there for a private girls-only New Year's Eve soiree—wore glittering clothes and party hats and clutched champagne flutes in their manicured hands. All that was lacking was a festive mood. Haley didn't feel as if she'd walked into a party; she felt as if she'd just walked into the war room at the Pentagon.

"You're involved as much as any of us," Coco said, waving her cell phone with a picture of Reese and one of his buxom new female friends in Haley's face. Haley cringed at the painful sight.

"But I have to admit that knowing those boys as I do, Spencer is probably the worst offender," Coco went on. "How dare he be so disloyal to me? In front of other people? Obviously you can't go anywhere or do anything in public that people won't find out about. Camera phones are everywhere—what moron doesn't know that? But if he thinks he's going to get away with this, he's even more of a devil than I thought. Those boys tricked us into thinking they were going on a wholesome family vacation, and then we see this!"

She waved another picture at the girls, this one of Spencer licking a blond girl's stomach. Yecch.

"I want revenge!" Coco cried. Her fine-boned face contorted with anger, but her chic gold-sequined minidress still complemented her curvy frame and brunette hair, carefully highlighted with autumnal reds and golds.

"Slow down, Coco," Sasha said. "Deep breaths."

"How can you be so calm, Sasha?" Coco said. "Look what your boyfriend is doing!"

Sasha had to turn her face away from a picture of her boyfriend, Johnny Lane, helping one of the girls tie—or untie, it was hard to tell the difference—the string on her bikini top.

"I know, I know," Sasha said. "Believe me, I'm furious too. But I don't want to rush into any crazy revenge scenarios. We need to think carefully before we act or we might do something we regret."

"Sasha's right," Whitney chimed in.

Coco mocked her. "'Sasha's right.' Of course you'd say that, Whit. Now that you and Sasha are practically sisters, you're like her walking echo."

Whitney's mother, Linda Klein, was living with Sasha's father, Jonathan Lewis. The relationship was looking very serious, so Sasha and Whitney—who'd always run in the same circle but had never really been on the same wavelength—had learned to overlook their differences. Differences which were considerable: Whitney was a bubbly fashionista—in fact, she designed and made all her own clothes—with highlighted blond hair, a fuller figure and an obsession with her weight. Sasha was a tall, leggy golden girl, a soccer star and singer/songwriter with long wavy hair and easy, effortless style. The two had become as close as sisters, which they now practically were, and this seemed to annoy Coco, who, as the third in their trio, was beginning to feel left out.

"Coco, you're just being mean," Cecily Watson said. Cecily was friendly with Coco but not always part of her inner circle, though she was certainly pretty enough to be one of the elite: tall, dark-skinned and graceful, with a funky sense of style.

"And besides, Whitney," Coco finished, ignoring Cecily, "you're the only one of us who doesn't have a boyfriend down in the Caribbean having an orgy with swimsuit models. So you can keep your mouth shut until we figure this out."

Whitney obediently held her tongue, and no one else came to her defense. Everybody knew Coco well enough to know that it was no use reasoning with her when she was this worked up—it would only invite her wrath. And no one wanted to be the object of Coco's unbridled ire.

"Somehow, I have a feeling Mia is behind all of this," Sasha said as she flicked through the photos. Mia Delgado was a Spanish supermodel who had spent some time at Hillsdale High chasing after her ex-boyfriend, Spanish exchange student Sebastian Bodega. Sebastian had decided to spend the term in Spain, claiming they couldn't bear another cold New Jersey winter. But, as far as anyone knew, they'd both be back come spring.

"That would be the absolute last straw," Cecily said.

"Why isn't Matt Graham in any of these pictures?" Whitney asked. "Isn't he one of Spencer's best friends?" Matthew Graham was a bad-boy buddy of Spencer's from his boarding school days. They'd both been kicked out, and now Matt went to Ridgewood, Hillsdale's rival school.

"I think Matt and Spencer are on the outs," Coco said. "And besides, Mrs. Eton refused to invite Matt. She thinks he's a bad influence on sweet little Spencey. If only she knew! She's going to lose it when she sees these pictures."

"Do you think she'll punish him somehow?" Haley asked.

"Who knows?" Coco said. "I don't care if she does or not. I don't leave punishment to amateurs."

Haley glanced nervously around the room, and caught the other girls doing the same. Coco could be a little scary when she decided to go for blood.

"Maybe you think the boys have some excuse for these pictures, some logical explanation?" Coco ranted. "You're in denial, girls! Look at these pictures. Really take them in. Think of all the awful things our boyfriends did with them! Look at them! Would any guy in his right mind be able to resist them?"

"What about a blind guy?" Whitney asked. Coco glared at her, nostrils flaring. "Never mind," Whitney said. "I'll shut up."

"Think about it," Coco went on. "Right now it's midnight down there, New Year's Eve. The guys are at a beach resort without their girlfriends. There are hot models in every direction, wearing practically nothing but a piece of dental floss. It's not only socially acceptable to kiss at midnight, girls, it's practically the law! What do you think is going to happen once those boys lock lips? Do you think they're going to stop right there and say, 'Okay, happy new year, I better get to bed now, good night'?"

There was silence for five full minutes while the girls—Coco, Haley, Sasha and Cecily—stared at the proof of their boyfriends' betrayal. Coco focused on the nightmarish Spencer pictures, while Sasha fixated on Johnny, Cecily on her longtime boyfriend, Drew Napolitano, and Haley on her cute and previously noble neighbor, Reese Highland.

Reese, she thought sadly. *What's happened to you?* Even with the hard evidence in front of her, she still had trouble believing her virtuous Reese could be this devilish.

Cecily broke the silence. "We've got to get them back for this. But what can we do? I don't know how to be that terrible."

"Well, luckily I do," Coco said. "Here's what we do. As soon as they get back from their little Caribbean jaunt, we execute a group dumping. We dump every single one of them at the same time, publicly, so that everybody, everywhere knows about it. Spencer Eton, Drew Napolitano, Johnny Lane and Reese Highland—jilted! That should humiliate them enough to make them see the error of their ways."

Haley felt doubtful. "What if that's not enough?" she said. "What if they don't really care?"

"We'll make them care," Coco said. "We'll—" She stopped, glancing at her vibrating phone. "Well, if it isn't Spencer Eton texting me with an innocent little New Year's greeting. How fricking sweet! What a fricking hypocrite!"

She paused to read the message and snapped the phone shut, looking shaken.

"What did he say?" Whitney asked.

"It's about the inaugural ball," Coco said. Haley knew Coco had been looking forward to that ball since the day Spencer's mother announced that she was running for governor of New Jersey. "Spencer says he can't wait to take me with him. It will be my official coming-out as First Girlfriend." Her face hardened, stricken with pain. "What a fraud! He probably had his tongue down some other girl's throat while he was pressing Send!"

"Well, so what?" Whitney said. "You're still going to go, aren't you? You're not going to miss the ball?"

"Only someone who doesn't have a boyfriend would say something like that," Coco snapped, and Whitney's face fell. "I don't want to miss the ball, but how can I go? After he has treated me so horrendously? I'm so disgusted I can't even look at him, much less appear in public with the snake."

This sounded new to Haley, who had always been under the impression that Coco was able to swallow any amount of personal pride for the sake of public appearances. Was Coco finally going to stand up to high society for the sake of her own sense of self? Whatever was going on, Haley had learned the valuable lesson Whitney hadn't yet seemed to master—don't contradict the queen when she's on a rampage. Besides, maybe Coco had changed, and in pointing this out, Haley might risk changing her back.

"Stupid Spencer," Coco muttered. "It's so unfair. And what really burns me up is that half of New Jersey gets to go, but not me! I was supposed to be the First Girlfriend! I mean, even geekoids like Mrs. Eton's lame new intern, what's-his-name, get to go."

"Alex Martin?" Haley said. She didn't consider Alex a geek—not really—but she knew he had been working for Mrs. Eton.

"Yes, that nerdinger," Coco said. "Well, this is it, girls. Things have to change. From this moment on, everything is going to be different around here."

She marched across the room and grabbed a stack of fashion magazines from the towering pile on her reading table. With a look of grim vengeance, she passed one to each of her friends. "One for you, one for you . . ."

"Oooh, oooh, oooh! Are we doing makeovers? Already?" Whitney squealed. "Goody!"

"More than just makeovers," Coco said. "This is a

complete and total overhaul. We are going to convert ourselves from hot suburban girls to completely irresistible world-class beauties, so that those boys really ache when they see what they're missing."

Cecily glanced at the cover of a teen magazine Coco had just given her. "'New Year, New You'?" she sniffed. "They do these stories every January, and there's never a new me."

"That's because you always quit after the third day, all of you," Coco chided. "This time's going to be different. This time, we're going to stick to the plan."

"I'm not sure I want to create a new me," Sasha said. "I kind of like the regular old me."

"Listen to me, girls," Coco said. "We're at our peak. This is the time when we define what the rest of our lives will be. When we start as little caterpillars in cocoons and emerge as gorgeous butterflies. This is the most crucial moment of our lives! In their own lame way, those boys have given us a gift. They've inspired us to become the best we can be. Sure, we're cute little high school girls now. But we can be better! Supermodel better. And when those idiot boys see what they're missing, they're going to eat their pitiful little hearts out."

"And then we'll take them back?" Cecily asked skeptically.

"No," Coco said. "That's when we really crush them, grind the stilettos into their hearts. We don't need those pathetic high school jocks. We can do a lot better than that. We're going to become the most glamorous creatures Hillsdale's ever seen. Boys will flock to us."

"Don't they already do that?" Cecily asked.

"I'm telling you, there will be no looking back," Coco commanded.

"But what other boys are there?" Sasha asked. "I mean, our guys are the best ones we know."

"There are better options out there," Coco said. "There have to be."

The girls shifted uncomfortably in their cushy seats. Haley was finding Coco's rant painful yet also curiously cathartic.

"Sasha, think about all the heartbreak Johnny's caused you over the past year or so," Coco said. "The fights. The misunderstandings. All the times he held you back from doing things you really wanted to do. Don't you deserve someone who'll worship you like the goddess you are—or will be, after I'm done with you?"

"Uh, I guess so," Sasha said. "But some of that Johnny stuff was because I—"

"Quiet," Coco snapped. "And Cecily," she went on. "Sure, Drew's attractive, in a meathead sort of way." Cecily gasped. "But he's not exactly the sharpest knife in the drawer. Meanwhile, look at you: you're beautiful, you're head cheerleader as a junior, you're a track star and you're smart enough to apply to the Ivies next year. Shouldn't you be with a guy who can live up to all that? Or will you settle for a dumb jock who's going to come back from college two years from now with a beer belly?"

"Well, when you put it that way . . . ," Cecily said.

"And you, Haley." Coco was on a roll now. "I'll admit that in some ways Reese Highland is untouchable. Yes, he's gorgeous and smart and a star athlete. And he always seemed to be such a good guy. But now look at him: parade a swimsuit model in front of him and he can't keep his filthy hands off her. Ask yourself, Haley: how well do you really know Reese? To me, these pictures say none of us ever knew him very well at all. He's got a secret dark side, and that's not what you deserve."

"Well, I am disappointed in him, it's true," Haley said. She had trusted Reese, she'd believed in him, and now she did doubt his integrity. Not only that, she wondered if he ever really cared about her in the first place or if he was just stringing her along.

"In a way, this is our own fault," Coco said. "We haven't been living up to our own fabulous potential. But that's all going to change, starting tonight." She began paging through a magazine, searching for ideas. "When those boys get back to Hillsdale, we are going to look hotter than they've ever seen us. They're going to drop to their knees. And that's when we're going to deliver the knee to the face. Boys, get ready to face the dumping squad!"

Coco raised her champagne flute. The other girls followed suit. "This is it, girls. New year, new you, new boys!"

"New year, new you, new boys!" echoed Whitney, Cecily, Sasha and Haley. They all clinked glasses.

Coco pointed them all to an article called "The Ultimate Detox." "I'm going to start with this," she announced. "Starting tomorrow I'm on a ten-day juice cleanse. It's the perfect new beginning. I'll purge myself of toxins—including the toxic bachelor Spencer Eton—and lose a quick few diet-starter pounds in the bargain. It's win-win. Who's with me?"

Sasha took the magazine and read about the benefits of the cleanse. "'Follow this regime to the letter and you'll have more energy than you ever thought possible, skin like a newborn baby's, brighter eyes, a stronger immune system, greater mental clarity, increased self-confidence and, on top of everything else, the pounds will just fall away.' Sounds almost like magic."

"I know," said Coco. "And it's going to change our lives."

• • •

New year, new you . . . it's a natural way to feel on January 1. But isn't Coco taking this spirit to the extreme? Maybe that's the only option when your boyfriend has just been caught snuggling with supermodels in the

Caribbean. If you're going to make a change, why not go all the way?

But will Haley decide to go along with this extreme regime? And if so, how far will she take it?

There's a big question looming here: why was Haley invited to join this little dinner party so late in the game? The most powerful clique at Hillsdale High—the Coco-Whitney-Sasha triumvirate—has officially reunited, taking Cecily Watson as its chosen mascot. So if three is a crowd, and four is a nice round number, what's five? Now that the Cocopuffs are back together and have adopted Cecily, will there be room in the power circle for Haley to take a seat?

The one thing Coco demands from her acolytes is that they conform to her sense of fabulousness. Haley can do that if she tries hard enough. The question is, does she want to? What does she have to gain, and what does she have to lose?

If you think Haley had better try harder to fit in with Coco's crowd before Cecily edges her out, turn to page 80, THE COCO CLEANSE.

When you throw in your lot with Coco, it's all or nothing. If you don't do things Coco's way, first she gets mad and then she gets even. If you think Haley isn't so sure about the crazy fad diets and bizarre skin care rituals—which might not be the healthiest path to take, especially given Coco's history of extreme control issues—have Haley approach EVERYTHING IN

MODERATION on page 76. She'll risk losing her place in the Hillsdale pecking order, but she has to ask herself if popularity is worth the high price.

Coco may be the most powerful girl at Hillsdale High, but she's not the only game in town. Alex Martin is interning at the governor's mansion, and that comes with a power of its own—power that goes way beyond the machinations of Hillsdale High. The fact that Alex is smart enough to land a plum internship with Mrs. Eton is impressive, and the inaugural ball is sure to be the social event of the season whether Coco De Clerq is in attendance or not. Besides, Alex does have a certain conservative charm, and Haley knows for a fact he has a soft spot for her. If you think Haley should find out what really goes on at the governor's mansion, turn to page 69, POLITICAL PREP, and help Alex set up for the big inaugural ball.

Lots of people resolve to improve themselves around the new year, but those resolutions don't always stick. This is Haley's chance to make some real changes in her life, to decide who she is and who she wants to be. Some of those changes are bound to be permanent, so choose carefully, or Haley could end up wishing she'd spent New Year's Eve at home alone with a pint of ice cream.

TRIPLE DATE

You don't need subtitles to read the writing on the wall.

"Want to hear the latest Darcy dirt?" Irene asked, barely able to contain herself.

"Ugh, not really," Haley said, but she leaned forward anyway. Haley had stopped in at Hap's Diner for a grilled cheese sandwich on her way home from returning an unwanted Christmas sweater. Now that Gam Polly had a full-time boyfriend, she was too busy to knit any more of her infamous barnyard-creature sweaters, which was a good thing. Unfortunately, she still liked to give presents. Gam had gotten the idea that puce was the "in" color for spring this year, and had sent sweaters for the entire family in that unflattering hue. Both of Haley's parents were too busy to drive her to the mall that afternoon to exchange hers, so Haley had to take the bus. She couldn't wait until she could finally get her driver's license—only a month or so away.

The mall had been a zoo, so Haley decided she needed fortification before making her way back to Camp Tofu, otherwise known as home. Irene happened to be at Hap's with her boyfriend, Shaun Willkommen, sharing a milk shake. Actually, Irene was sharing one of Shaun's three milk shakes. Now that Shaun was on the track team, he had an excuse to eat like a bear. Haley perched next to them at the counter.

"I don't see what's so terrible about Darcy," Shaun said. "She's always nice to me."

Irene rolled her eyes. "You're such a boy."

Shaun grinned and rubbed his blond crew cut. "What's wrong with that?"

"I'll tell you what's wrong with it," Irene said. "Boys never see past the surface of things. They're too easily fooled."

Shaun shrugged and slurped his vanilla shake. "Whatever works. If being a girl means analyzing every move some chick makes and dreaming up a scheme to go with it, I'll stay on Boy Island, thanks. Dang if I gots the energy."

"What are you talking about?" Haley said. "You've got more energy than anyone I know. By the way, I saw you on Channel Seven News last week. Nice parallel parking job."

Shaun had ridden his father's lawn mower into Manhattan and parked it in front of Radio City Music Hall before going in to see the Christmas show. A news van spotted him and interviewed him, then filmed him driving the mower into the mouth of the Lincoln Tunnel.

"What can I say? I love the Rockettes." That was Shaun's idea of an explanation.

"Ugh," Irene said. "Darcy's cheap tricks are starting to work on Devon. Do you know, yesterday she waltzed into Jack's and told Devon that a movie scout had approached her about playing a teen runaway, and so she needed a sexy costume for the audition?" Devon, everyone knew, worked part-time at Jack's Vintage Clothing to earn extra money, and Haley had often invented her own clothing needs just to have an excuse to stop by and see him. "He spent hours helping her try on trashy clothes, and meanwhile the whole story turned out to be a big fat lie."

"So she bogused a movie deal to hang with the guy," Shaun said. "Eiggib on."

"Ugh!" Irene gasped, exasperated. Even Haley knew Shaun well enough by now to know that "Eiggib on" was backwards for "No biggie." Shaun liked to talk backwards occasionally. It was one of his quirks. "Darcy never comes out and says she wants to be with Devon. She's always got some phony reason she has to be near him. It's totally manipulative. And it's working. Devon's at the point now that whenever we ask him to do something his first response is 'Sure, I'll see if Darcy can come.' And you think I like hanging out with that little pervy twerp?"

"This is worse than I thought." Haley put down her sandwich. She'd been feeling kind of territorial toward Devon in the past few days, thinking she should be the one cooing over veggie dumplings with him, not Darcy Podowski. But she'd always figured that sooner or later, he'd get tired of Darcy's tricks and come to his senses. Lately, though, it was abundantly clear that Darcy was actually getting to Devon; she was a real threat, and it was time for Haley to quit fooling around and step up to the challenge.

"Take my advice, Haley," Irene said. "Make an effort here, or you'll lose Devon to Darcy for good. And nobody wants to see that happen. Certainly not me and Shaun."

"Speak for yourself, woman. I dig the pervy twerp." Irene punched him in the shoulder. "Okay, fine, you want to worm your way into their little mud hut and cool down whatever's been heating up between 'em, I get it." Haley and Irene stared at

Shaun, surprised. "What? I listen, I pay attention. I can scheme with the best of them. I happen to think it's a huge waste of milliseconds, but . . ."

"Shaun the love guru," Irene said.

"No, no, maybe he's right," Haley said. "You know, keep your friends close, and keep your enemies—"

"On a choke leash chained to the garage," Shaun interrupted. "That's right."

"You aren't seriously thinking of listening to him, are you?" Irene asked.

"What else am I supposed to do? Devon and Darcy are probably doing it as we speak."

"If that's the case, they got one interesting mating dance," Shaun said. "They're coming this way. Ti t'nsi, ecnedicnioc ynnuf a s'taht?"

"It's a small town, Shaun," Haley said.

"Too small," Irene added.

Devon and Darcy strolled into the diner and waved at Irene, Shaun and Haley. Devon started toward them to say hello, but Darcy grabbed his sleeve and said, "Quick! A booth just opened up!" and dragged him away.

"See what I mean?" Irene said.

"That was cold," Shaun said. "Let a guy say yo-yo to his friends, at least, before you give him the cat's cradle."

Haley finished her sandwich, trying not to glance

in Devon's direction. But she didn't need to look—Shaun was happy to give her the play-by-play.

"Devon started to sit down across from Darcy, but she's making him sit on the same side as her," Shaun said. "Here comes the waitress with their water . . . ooh! Darcy's pulling the old 'I spilled water on my T-shirt' trick. 'Devon, will you help me wipe it off?'" Shaun put on a girly voice for Darcy's lines, then switched to a deep boy voice. "'Sure, Darcy, anything for you. . . .'"

"We don't need you to do the voices, Dr. Seduction," Irene said. "I feel like I'm listening to a puppet show."

"Now they're ordering. . . . Darcy's saying, 'I'll have a big heaping helping of Devon! Mmm . . . mmm . . . good.'"

"Okay, Shaun, that's enough," Irene said. "Haley, time to make your move. Why don't you amble on over there and ask the two of them if they want to do something this weekend? Say, go to the Strand to see the latest foreign film? I believe they're showing *Days of the Sun, Nights of the Moon*. It's in Russian. Devon will love it, and Darcy won't be able to get past the subtitles. It's perfect."

Haley couldn't miss the wicked grin on Irene's face. "Good idea. I've seen it ten times. It's part of my dad's permanent archives." She got up and straightened her skirt.

Shaun used his girly voice again: "Now Darcy's

saying, 'Hey Devon, want to see my latest piercing? Bet you can't guess where it is. . . .'"

"Quit it, Shaun," Irene said.

Haley walked over to the booth and slid in across from Devon and Darcy. "Hey, guys," she said casually. "What's up?"

"Just ordering some chow," Devon said.

"I'm addicted to the fries here," Darcy said.

"They're great, aren't they?" Haley said. "You know, I don't get to see you guys enough. Want to go to a movie this weekend, just the three of us?"

Darcy's eyes narrowed. But Devon said, "Sure, that's cool. Whatevs."

"Awesome," Haley said. "Why don't you guys meet me at the Strand tomorrow night at eight? I'll get the tickets. My treat."

"The Strand?" Darcy said. "What's playing there, some foreign crap?"

"That's my favorite theater," Devon said, clearly wounded.

"I know," Haley said brightly, smiling at Darcy.

Just then, the waitress arrived with their food, so Haley hopped up to go. "So we'll see you tomorrow," Devon confirmed as Haley walked away. And she couldn't help but notice he seemed just the slightest bit sad to see her go.

Back on her stool at the counter, Haley triumphantly announced, "Phase one of the mission accomplished."

Shaun rubbed his hands together with glee. "E-e-e-excellent."

"There's three seats together." Haley pointed toward a section in the middle of the small theater. Not that the place was all that crowded.

"Why couldn't we see *Zombie Rampage* instead?" Darcy said. "I heard it was awesome."

"This film's very uplifting," Haley said. "You'll see." She was hoping Devon would see too—see how shallow and immature Darcy was. So far he appeared to be fairly clueless on that front.

Darcy slid into the row first. Haley cut in front of Devon so that she could sit between the two of them, on Darcy's right. But Darcy patted the seat to her left and said, "Sit here, Dev. It's closer to the middle of the screen."

Devon slid past Haley and sat on the other side of Darcy. Darcy looked at Haley and smiled. "There. We'll all be much more comfortable this way."

The lights went dim and the trailers played. *That little sneak,* Haley thought, barely noticing what was happening on the screen in front of her. Not that it mattered—she had the movie practically memorized. *Irene was right—I never realized how manipulative Darcy really is.*

The first scene opened with ominous orchestral music. Credits were written in Russian and translated below. The main character, a farmer, appeared, speaking incomprehensible gibberish. The subtitles flashed below him.

Darcy chomped her gum and sighed. "I can't believe we have to sit here and read the movie. What a drag!"

That's right, Haley thought. *Keep showing your true colors.* She leaned back in her seat and settled in for two hours of Russian tragedy in the steppes. She tried to keep an eye on Devon and Darcy, but the film was actually pretty absorbing, even on the eleventh viewing, though admittedly not as action-packed as *Zombie Rampage* would have been. Every once in a while she glanced over at the couple. Darcy was rubbing Devon's hand and popping her gum, completely ignoring the screen, while Devon stared up at the movie in a kind of spaced-out trance.

When the film ended, Darcy sprang to her feet and announced, "Thank God that's over. Let's get out of here."

Devon frowned.

"Wow, that was so intense. I think I've . . . I should visit the restroom and collect my thoughts," Haley said pensively. Devon nodded as if he understood. "I'll meet you in the lobby," she said, heading for the ladies' room alone. However, when she came out of the stall to wash her hands, she found Darcy by the sinks reapplying her blue eyeliner.

"Thanks for inviting us to the movie," Darcy said. "Even though it sucked."

"Sorry you didn't like it," Haley said.

"I don't know what you think you're trying to pull," Darcy said. "But it didn't work. And it never will."

"I wasn't trying to pull anything," Haley said, her hackles up.

"It's sad, really. I feel sorry for you, Haley. Deeply sorry."

"Sorry for me?" Haley said. "Why?"

Darcy didn't look away from the mirror, but kept slathering on eyeliner. "It's so obvious how much you like Devon. Like, it couldn't be more obvious. But it's just as obvious that he only likes you as a friend. You'd have to be totally delusional not to see it."

Haley was stunned. How could this girl speak so bluntly to her? Darcy was calling her delusional?

"You're the delusional one," Haley said, struggling to keep her voice from cracking. "If you think someone as shallow as you will ever be able to keep Devon's interest for longer than a nanosecond."

Darcy laughed. "You're crazy. He's totally into me. You're just some homely classmate."

Homely? That was it. The gloves were off.

"We'll see about that," Haley said, glaring at her opponent.

"Yeah, we will." Darcy flounced out of the bathroom. Haley stayed by the sink for another minute composing herself. When she came out and looked for Devon and Darcy, they were gone.

So that's how it is, Haley thought. She gritted her teeth as she walked home in the cold. Now she saw Darcy for who she really was: a fierce competitor for Devon's affections.

She'd better be ready, Haley thought. *Because I'm not going to give up without a fight.*

It's on.

• • •

So Darcy's dark side has come out—in all its Technicolor glory. Haley's all worked up at the moment, but will the feeling last? Once she has time to mull things over, will she still want to head into an all-out war with the bleached blond frosh?

If you think this nasty little bathroom run-in has fired Haley up for good, have her rise to the challenge and compete for Devon's heart on page 84, FORMIDABLE OPPONENT.

There are other things going on in Haley's life, though—a lot of other things. One of the biggest events in her life is her upcoming driver's test, and the possibility of that car her parents mentioned on New Year's. Haley won't pass the test unless she practices, and to practice she needs to focus on driving, not boy troubles

and catfights. If you're sure Haley cares more about getting her license than beating Darcy at her own game, go to page 95, DRIVING PRACTICE.

Finally, all this drama is enough to make a girl's head spin. To have Haley just head home to clear her head before deciding what to do next, go to page 118, ON THE SCALE.

Haley's got a lot on her plate right now. It's up to you to help her decide what's important and keep her priorities straight.

VON-METZGER

A happy occasion for some can be brutally painful for others.

Haley arrived at the Von-Metzger household to find the festivities in full swing under a makeshift tent in the backyard. Rick Von, art teacher extraordinaire, had gone all out to celebrate his recent engagement to Dave Metzger's mother, Nora. The tent looked homemade—like no party structure Haley had ever seen, in fact—but it was beautifully lit up with twinkling lights, like a swarm of winter fireflies. A space heater kept the area warm in spite of the January chill. Picnic tables covered with colorful Indian fabrics acted as banquet tables, and Mrs. Metzger had set candles and bowls of amaryllis all around.

"Welcome, Haley," Mr. Von said in his soft, gentle voice. "Do you know, I made this tent myself."

"Oh, I never would have guessed!" Haley exclaimed after offering Mr. Von her congratulations.

"Yes, I fashioned it out of my favorite old clothes and vintage cloth I've collected over the years. I wanted everything at the party to have meaning, even the fabric that surrounds us."

"Um, that's a lovely sentiment," Haley said, trying her best to be polite.

"Right this way to the gift station," Mr. Von said, leading Haley to a table covered with paints, brushes and paper. "In lieu of gifts we ask each of our guests to paint us a portrait of our love." Haley saw a middle-aged woman with wild gray hair, busy painting a picture of a cactus.

"That's . . . a lovely sentiment," Haley repeated, now slightly creeped out. How was she supposed to know what Mr. Von and Mrs. Metzger's love looked like?

She had to admit that she'd never seen her eccentric art teacher look so happy, or so neat. Since Nora Metzger had moved in, Mr. Von's shirts were actually clean, ironed and even starched. Mrs. Metzger couldn't seem to do much with her son's hygiene habits, but she'd made a big improvement in Mr. Von's.

Over by the hors d'oeuvre table, the usual art-student crowd had gathered, including Irene Chen and Shaun Willkommen, though there was no sign of Devon McKnight and his now-constant companion, Darcy Podowski. Dave, Annie and Hannah were huddled around the refreshments table sipping punch, and Alex Martin was talking to a strange man Haley didn't recognize. *So he made it after all,* Haley thought. Alex had been so busy with preparations for Eleanor Eton's inauguration lately, it had seemed doubtful that he would make an appearance. With his graying Vandyke beard and white Southern Gentleman suit flecked with paint, the stranger looked like someone who might have gone to art school with Mr. Von. The rest of the guests were arty friends of Rick's and suburby friends of Nora's, two subsets that didn't intersect very much, Haley noticed.

Haley got herself a glass of punch and went over to congratulate Dave, who was now loitering near the entrance of the tent as if to prepare himself for a speedy exit. "Hey, Dave, how are you holding up?"

"Fine. Fine. Fine. Fine," Dave said nervously.

"You seem a little tense," Haley said. "I can certainly understand that. But Mr. Von's not a bad guy. I bet once you get used to having him around you'll grow to really—"

"That's not what's making me tense," Dave said. "It's RoBro! He's in a very fragile state right now."

Haley sensed Dave was projecting. "So it's official? RoBro! has been unveiled?"

"We prefer the word *born,*" Dave insisted. "Ro-Bro! was just born yesterday. Twenty pounds, five ounces, thirty-four inches tall."

"Congratulations. You're a brother!"

Dave smiled nervously. "Thank you. I'm excited. I really love the little guy. You should see him now, Haley. He's so adorable and he says the cutest things."

"Really? I would like to see him."

"But I worry about him. I'm afraid Hannah and I might have let him be born prematurely. That's why I have to check on him every fifteen minutes, to make sure he's warm enough, getting enough electricity and functioning properly."

"I see." Poor Dave was really losing it over this robot brother of his. Haley remembered what it was like to be an only child—she was nine when her brother, Mitchell, was born—and frankly, she'd never minded one bit being the only child in the house. It was little brothers who were the pain in the neck. Why would you want to create one if you didn't have to?

Haley heard the *ding-ding-ding* sound of fork against glass and turned to see Mr. Von standing on a chair, trying to get the party's attention.

"My dear friends and companions in life's long and mysterious journey," he said. "I'd like to take a moment to say a few words." The guests quieted down and gathered around Mr. Von. "The day I met

Nora is the day my life turned around," he said. "She's the paint, I'm the brush, and together we're creating a beautiful canvas of our lives."

"Awww," said a few people in the crowd.

"And so, as you all know, I asked Nora to join me on life's meandering road, to take my hand in marriage. To my great honor, she accepted."

Everyone clapped.

"And now I'd like to ask someone else to join us on our cosmic trip through the universe," Mr. Von continued. "Dave, would you come up here?"

Dave looked at Haley in terror, his hands shaking violently. "Go on, he won't bite you. He's vegetarian," Haley said, nudging Dave toward his stepfather-to-be.

Dave stood in front of Mr. Von as Nora took her son's shaking hand. "David, tonight I ask you if you would do me the great honor of becoming my son." Mr. Von raised his glass. "Dave, will you become our Dave Metzger-Von or Dave Von-Metzger? Whichever you prefer."

Nora beamed at Dave and squeezed his hand. Dave's eyes widened; he stared around the tent as if at a tribunal announcing his death sentence. *An overreaction, sure,* Haley thought. But maybe Mr. Von shouldn't have sprung this on a temperamental guy like Dave in public.

"What do you say, Dave?" Mr. Von made a toasting motion with his glass, and the rest of the crowd followed suit. "To David Metzger-Von or Von-Metzger!"

People clinked glasses and drank while Dave stammered, "Um—um—I've got s-something to do." He dashed through the mob of guests and disappeared into the garage. Nora looked concerned as she watched him go.

"He's just checking on RoBro!" Haley assured her. "He'll be back."

"Who?" Nora said, and Haley realized she had no idea what Haley was talking about.

More platters of food appeared, and soon everybody at the party was busy eating, drinking and chatting. Haley sat down at a picnic table with Annie, Alex, Irene, Shaun and a plateful of dilled salmon on pumpernickel.

"Has Dave come back from the garage yet?" she asked.

"No, I haven't seen him," Alex said.

"He and Hannah won't stop fussing with that RoBro!" Annie said. "I'm starting to worry about him. Them. Well, mostly Dave."

"You're just starting to worry about him?" Irene said. "The guy's been off his chair from day one."

"What's this Bro-Ro yous keep talking about?" Shaun asked. "And when can I meet him?"

"I wish Dave would get back here," Annie said. "He's missing the whole party."

"I think that may be the point," Alex offered.

"Maybe something's really wrong with RoBro!" Haley said, shrugging.

"RoBro!?" Shaun asked. "Or is it orBoR!?"

"I'm going to go check on him," Annie said.

"I'll come with you," Haley said.

"I'll go too," Alex said.

"And we'll stay here and eat," Irene said. "If it's all the same to you."

Haley, Alex and Annie made their way out to the garage, but Dave wasn't there. He was in the driveway with Hannah. RoBro! was lying flat on his back in an old red wagon, hooked up to the battery of Annie's electric car by an array of colorful cables.

"Dave, what are you doing?" Haley asked.

"Giving him a transfusion," Dave said. "He needs constant energy or he fades away. I need to resuscitate him!"

"Thanks for asking my permission, Dave," Annie said. "You're going to drain my battery. How am I supposed to get home?"

"I'll recharge it," Dave promised. He and Hannah returned to their emergency surgery as Annie, Haley and Alex plopped down on the curb.

"Your car is really sweet, Annie," Haley said. "I hope my parents will let me have something like this for my birthday."

"Have you been practicing for that driving test?"

Annie asked. "Because I'm telling you, it's a bear. It's harder than AP Calculus, AP Trigonometry and AP Physics combined."

"Actually, I've hardly had any practice time at all," Haley said. "My parents are always too busy to take me out driving. I don't think they realize how soon my birthday is coming up."

"Don't worry, Haley," Alex said. "You'll do great on your driving test. I've always admired your hand-eye coordination."

"Wow. Thanks." It was a strange sort of compliment, but Haley felt her face warm pleasantly. Alex was, after all, incredibly cute, and a senior, and a shoo-in to be named Most Likely to Succeed.

"Are you serious? You absolutely need to practice," Annie exclaimed. "In fact, I'll help you. Whenever you want. Just let me know."

"Thanks, Annie." Haley was slightly disappointed. She'd been hoping Alex would offer to take her out for a spin.

"Well, it sounds like you'll be pretty busy with all the driving," Alex said, "but I could really use some help with the preparations for the inaugural ball, if you can spare the time."

"Could you please keep it down?" Dave said. "RoBro! needs his rest, and you're exciting him."

Haley glanced at Alex, who made a "don't say it" face. Haley said it anyway.

"I think Dave's mother's engagement is really getting to him," she whispered to Annie. "Like in a it's-time-for-therapy sort of way." Annie nodded reluctantly.

"Mr. Von's toast didn't help," Alex said. "Dave has already made it abundantly clear he doesn't want to be Dave Von-Metzger. So why don't his mom and soon-to-be-stepfather know that?"

"I just hope Mr. Von doesn't press the issue," Haley said with a sideways glance at Dave, who was patting RoBro!'s face as if the machine were a living, breathing, sleeping child. "Dave seems to be acting out some deep-seated family issues."

"You're not kidding," Annie whispered. "Yesterday he called me Mom."

● ● ●

Dave seems to be on the brink of the deep end, but then, he often seems that way. Something—maybe the steady love of his girlfriend, Annie—always manages to pull him back from the edge just in time. Haley's sympathetic, but does she need to get on board this emotional roller coaster? She's got her own family and her own problems to deal with.

If you think Haley has put off learning to drive for long enough and had better get busy if she wants to get her license in February, send her off to page 95, DRIVING PRACTICE.

If you think Haley should start hanging with a more upscale crowd, have her go help Alex on page 101, INAUGURATION.

Lastly, if you think Haley needs a break from all this craziness and should take a five-minute chill, send her home on page 118, ON THE SCALE.

POLITICAL PREP

Politics makes strange bedfellows, but it makes even weirder friends with benefits.

Haley arrived at Alex's house ready to do whatever she could to help him get ready for the big inaugural ball; still, she wasn't expecting flash cards.

They took their coffee into the den, ready to work, and Alex handed her a big stack of photos—portraits of prominent people, with their names and notes about their political tastes and affiliations on the back. It was Haley's job to hold up the photos one at a time and quiz Alex on the details.

She flashed him a picture of a wrinkled, white-haired old man with a bow tie and cane.

"Eli Morgenstern," Alex said. "Republican, retired head of Morgenstern Investments . . ."

"Wife?" Haley prompted.

"Diana Rieff Morgenstern, on the board of the Philharmonic and the Museum of Modern Art, secret Democrat."

"Good." An important part of Alex's job was helping Mrs. Eton work the crowd at the ball, and to remember who was who in case she forgot a name or something important about a particular guest's background. Haley held up another photo, this one showing an elegant, thirtyish woman in a chignon and pearls.

"Carrie Sargent, a public relations executive . . ."

"Where?" Haley asked.

"Holland Associates?" Alex guessed.

"Right. Anything else about her?"

"Hmm, Sargent . . . Oh! Her father's head of the public TV station in the city."

"And?"

"And . . . her sister is a lawyer in the state's attorney general's office. The sister's name is . . . Martha Sargent Koppel."

"And?"

"And Carrie and Martha like to ride horses in Central Park."

"Excellent." Haley put the stack of pictures

down, having run through all of them twice. "You're in pretty good shape on guest trivia. What's next?"

"Tomorrow I'm confirming all the live music for inauguration day. What do you think of this lineup? The New Jersey Brass Orchestra for the ceremony itself, the Montclair String Quartet for the post-ceremony reception. Then, for the ball, the Joe Henderson Sextet during cocktails and dinner, Monty Mason's Swing Band for dancing—featuring Helen Taymor, this cabaret singer Mrs. Eton loves—followed by the Jazzcats for the wind-down. I tried to book Springsteen, but he said no."

"He's a famous Dem," Haley said.

Alex shrugged. "I had to give it a shot. This is Jersey, after all."

Haley laughed. "That sounds perfect—something for everyone except the punks and the rappers, who, come to think of it, probably won't be in attendance. Now what's this?" She pointed to a large sheet of paper diagrammed with numbered circles.

"Ugh, the seating chart," Alex said. "It's like a logic problem on the LSATs—impossible. Mrs. Eton wants to match charity heads with deep pockets, and sprinkle some local celebs generously throughout so that no one feels left out, and at the same time make sure no mortal enemies are seated together, near each other or in each other's sight lines across the crowded room."

"Sounds like fun," Haley said. "Let's get to

work." She picked up the guest list and started studying it. To her surprise, she recognized a lot of the names on it. Her mother had worked with a lot of the politicians, lawyers and businesspeople on the list, and her filmmaker father knew some of the local artists and arts administrators. Haley had absorbed information about these people by osmosis, just by sitting at the dinner table with her parents. She never realized how much she'd picked up from their conversations.

"Mort Jarvis thinks of himself as a philanthropist." Alex pointed to a name on the list. "He's loaded, and he likes to give to educational causes."

"Teresa Chandler," Haley said, picking out another name on the list. "She runs Princeton's financial aid office. Plus she just got divorced, and Mort Jarvis is a widower, isn't he?"

"Perfect," Alex said, jotting down notes. "We'll put them at table five, with the head of the Rutgers philosophy department and Alice Shaw, who gives a lot of money to the ballet."

"The Rutgers philosophy department—you mean Brian Hooper?" Haley asked. Alex nodded. "Those two can't be together. They used to date!"

"Whoops." Alex crossed out Alice Shaw. "What about Catherine Yardley? She's Mrs. Eton's press secretary."

"I guess that's okay," Haley said. "As long as she

doesn't bring up Mrs. Eton's cuts to the education budget."

"Don't worry, she won't," Alex said. "Everybody knows that's a touchy subject."

They worked their way through the guest list until all the tables were filled and all potential snubbings and feuds avoided. Haley insisted that Alex sample all the hors d'oeuvres the caterer was serving before the ball and that every vendor, from the decorator to the musicians, was triple-confirmed a week in advance to avoid unpleasant surprises.

"You're really amazing at this, Haley." Alex leaned back, tired and ready to relax. "I had no idea you knew so much about local politics."

"Ha," Haley said. "You know what? Neither did I!"

"Well, I'm impressed," Alex said. "I couldn't have pulled this off without you."

"Thanks," Haley said. "It was fun."

They retired to the kitchen. "I'm starving." Alex opened the freezer and pulled out a gallon of vanilla ice cream. "Join me in a hot fudge sundae?"

"Just what I'm in the mood for," Haley said. She scooped ice cream into bowls while Alex heated up the sauce.

"You do deserve a reward for helping me out," Alex said.

"Agreed," Haley said flirtatiously.

"The thing is, I had something a little more meaningful in mind," Alex said. "Haley, would you like to be my date to the inauguration? Before you say no, you pinko commie bleeding heart liberal, you should know you'd be doing me a huge favor, from heading off any unforeseen seating chart disasters, to helping me remember all those people on my flash cards."

"Is that the only reason you want me to go, my right wing neocon friend?" Haley asked, smirking.

"N-no," Alex stammered. "It's just, this whole event would be a lot more fun if you were by my side. There. I said it. So what do you say, Haley? Be my date?"

• • •

Wow, the inauguration! A high-profile, black-tie affair and probably the biggest social event of the year. That's some fancy date for our little Haley. But, as Alex said, she deserves to go after all the hard work she's done on the preparations. If you think Haley would love to go to the ball with Prince Alex, turn to page 101, INAUGURATION.

But is the inauguration really a romantic date, or is Alex just using Haley's sociopolitical smarts to make himself look good? Maybe you think Alex is not foremost in Haley's mind at the moment, and that other boys—namely one Reese Highland—have been secretly dominating her thoughts in recent days. Alex's offer is tempting, but if Haley lets too much time pass before

dealing with the Reese issue, he could slip through her fingers for good. If you think Haley needs to speak her mind to Reese and get a few things off her chest before she can move on, turn to page 112, MAN DOWN.

Finally, Haley must be wiped after all this volunteer work. To have her take a breather, send her home for a rest on page 118, ON THE SCALE.

EVERYTHING IN MODERATION

Sometimes extreme circumstances call for moderate measures.

"You're eating that?" Coco sniffed at the chicken breast and steamed broccoli Haley was eating for lunch. "You know what they say: a moment on the lips, a lifetime on the hips."

"It's a lean, skinless, broiled chicken breast with no sauce," Haley said. "It's almost pure protein. No carbs. Plus broccoli is, like, packed with vitamins and has almost zero calories. You can't get much less fattening than this."

"Whatever you say." Coco sipped her hot water with lemon.

It was the first day back at school after winter vacation. Haley had gotten up early that morning to go for a long run. It was freezing cold outside, but she had to admit she felt pretty great afterward, and her cheeks retained a rosy glow.

Coco's New Year's Eve speech had inspired her, in a way. She was furious with Reese for what he'd done in the Caribbean, and she wanted to be at her best when she confronted him. She also wanted to do something to boost her energy levels and to help herself feel better, so that Reese's betrayal wouldn't leave her feeling depressed. So, she was exercising more than usual, drinking a lot of water, eating more fruits and vegetables and cutting out foods that clouded up her system, like heavy sweets and simple starches in the packaged breads and crackers category. Overall, she thought she was doing pretty well. She'd shed three pounds of baby fat and was looking tall and lean, but still had respectable curves.

What she wasn't willing to do was take the Coco Cleanse, which, as far as Haley could tell, amounted to ingesting lots of hot water, lemon juice, cayenne pepper and little else. Even diet soda was off-limits, as Coco insisted it led to bloating and that the added chemicals weren't a friend to skin.

Now she and Coco were having lunch together in

the cafeteria, if you could call Coco's cup of water lunch. "You want a bite?" Haley offered her a piece of chicken.

Coco shook her head. "That's not on the Coco Cleanse. You're not following the regimen, and I hate to say it, Haley, but it totally shows." She pinched the skin on Haley's upper arm as an example.

Haley tried to keep her temper. "That's muscle," she said, seething.

Haley had a feeling that for Coco, this "healthy regimen" was really about deprivation, starvation and self-control, certainly not health. She accurately guessed it was a way for Coco to feel in charge after Spencer had pulled the sarong out from under her on his modelizing trip to Nevis. "I'm worried about you, Coco. I'm afraid you're taking this cleanse thing way, way too seriously."

Coco pulled a fashion magazine out of her bag and pointed to the model on the cover. "Look at her. Look how skinny she is! She makes me look like a total fatty. Apparently, this is the kind of girl Spencer likes, so that's what I'm going for. And I won't stop until I get there."

"You're pretty close already," Haley warned. Coco smiled with satisfaction, but that wasn't Haley's intended effect. She couldn't help but notice that her friend's skin and eyes were starting to look dull and tired. Coco seemed to have lost some of her fierce spirit and compelling edge. Sure, she could be a little too spirited at times, especially if you got on her bad side, but without that spark of personality, Coco was missing most of her overall appeal. How could Haley tell her that to her face without having her own head chopped off and served to her on a platter?

Now that most certainly was *not* a menu item on Coco's New Year's diet.

• • •

Coco has always had a tendency to go overboard, and this cleanse is no exception. It's as if she's lost all sense of proportion. If you think the waif look is in, turn to IV on page 121.

All the dieting and cleansing is for a purpose, don't forget: to make those flirty beach boys eat their hearts out. Looking lean and mean is just one part of the plan. If you want to see what goes down when the ladies unleash their arsenal of weapons on the unsuspecting boys, go to page 112, MAN DOWN.

Of course, changing your looks and getting revenge on unfaithful boys is risky business, best done carefully. If you think Haley should go home and regroup before she makes any major decisions about love and life, turn to page 118, ON THE SCALE.

Do boys really want girls who are literally starving for attention? Haley's about to find out.

THE COCO CLEANSE

If you are what you eat, what is a person who eats nothing?

"Everything with calories is bad for you," Coco declared.

"Even spinach?" Whitney said. "Even fish?"

"Everything," Coco said.

"That doesn't really make sense, Coco," Sasha protested. "Food is the fuel your body needs to get up in the morning and get through the day. Calories are just a measure of how much energy you'll get from your food."

"That's the sort of thing fat people say," Coco said. "So I'd expect it coming from you."

While Coco and the other girls were following a strict ten-day fasting plan—they were currently on day two—Sasha was still consuming some light proteins and steamed vegetables. And Coco wasn't letting her forget it, needling her constantly about her "chubby" cheeks and "thick" thighs, even though there was nothing chubby or thick about Sasha at all.

Haley had decided there was no arguing with the Gospel According to Coco, though. She'd been given a guest pass to Coco's health club, where all the other girls belonged, so that she could join her friends for a group "detox" sauna in the mornings before school. She loved how refreshed it made her feel. Her skin looked clearer and her mind felt sharper. But it also made her thirsty, like, really thirsty, and she drank gallons of water to make up for all the fluid she sweated out every morning.

"Food is the enemy," Coco went on. "All food."

"What about mangoes? Or grapefruit?" Whitney said. "I heard they speed your metabolism."

"You don't need to speed your metabolism if you haven't taken in any calories to burn," Coco said, leaning back against the cedar sauna wall and adjusting her towel.

"Can't argue with that," Cecily said.

"So what can we eat?" Whitney moaned. Giving up sweets had been the hardest for her.

"Nothing," Coco declared. "Except for lemon juice."

She really is serious, Haley thought. After all, even paramecia needed to eat something . . . bacteria, if Haley recalled last year's biology class correctly. No woman could live on lemon juice alone. And in fact, Haley had secretly been picking at healthy dinners with her family at night, and having two bites from a small bowl of oatmeal before school in the mornings. She'd expected the diet to last a couple of days and then for everyone to come to their senses, but Coco was showing no signs of letting up.

"Heat's the best thing for you," Coco said. "I basically live in heat now. Sauna in the morning, steam showers at night, Bikram yoga in the afternoons . . . it makes me feel great. All the gunk in my system is being flushed out. I think it's working, don't you?"

Cecily checked her watch. "That's twenty minutes. We ought to get to school."

The girls trooped into the locker room for cooling showers. Haley opened her locker, unscrewed the cap on a big bottle of water and drank it down as Coco took off her towel and started getting dressed. Haley noticed that her friend's normally svelte body was even tighter and firmer than usual. Coco was actually beginning to look like a swimsuit model—if the adage was true that the camera packed on ten pounds and those pounds were distributed in all the right places.

Haley glanced down at her own stomach, which felt puffier than ever, probably because she'd been drinking so much water. *The cleanse is working for Coco,* she thought. *Why isn't it working for me?*

• • •

If you think Haley should focus on Operation Dump 'Em and get the hard part over with, turn to page 112, MAN DOWN. If you want her to weigh in after all this cleansing effort to see if she's lost any pounds, flip to page 118, ON THE SCALE. Finally, if you think Haley is starting to think she might need to lose a few more pounds after seeing Coco's skinny frame, follow Coco's extreme diet lead on page 121, IV.

FORMIDABLE OPPONENT

Smart is not the same thing as wise.

"I can't believe Darcy said that to you," Irene said. "Not only is she a cheap flirt, she plays dirty!"

"She's even starting to annoy me," Shaun said. "And I'm usually a fan of pop tarts."

Haley was at Shaun's house recounting her disastrous triple date with Devon and Darcy. The story of Darcy assailing Haley in the bathroom really got them going. Haley was glad to have Shaun and Irene on her side when it came to Devon. Maybe they could help her get Darcy out of the way for good.

"She throws herself at him every chance she gets," Haley complained. "And he doesn't have a clue."

"She's got the blinders on him, for reals," Shaun said. "I don't mind having the ladies come a'calling, but we haven't given her the Willkommen seal of approval yet, and I can't recall the last time me and the Devster kicked it mano a mano."

"And have you noticed how any time there's even the remotest chance of rain she wears a white T-shirt? And 'forgets' her jacket?" Irene said. "Totally on purpose. I don't know why Devon can't see through her."

"Maybe because he can see through her shirt," Shaun joked.

Irene glared at him. "Shaun. Not funny."

"Saw ti thguoht I," Shaun replied.

"It's like she's got him under a spell," Haley said. "Do you think she's using black magic?"

"It must be the dark arts because Devon's not that dumb," Irene said. "At least, I never thought he was."

The doorbell rang. "Oh, who could that be?" Irene said sarcastically.

"Probably D-Squared," Shaun said.

"Well, aren't you going to answer it?" Irene asked.

"Let me get my monocle." Shaun had taken to wearing a monocle when greeting guests. Haley didn't know where this latest quirk came from—

apparently from some old British TV series he'd recently started watching—but Shaun was always up to some new weirdness; it hardly surprised Haley anymore.

Shaun found his monocle on the kitchen counter and answered the door with a British accent. "Willkommen to the Willkommen household. I'm the butler, Shaunessy. Do come in."

"Thanks, Shaun," Devon said, hardly batting an eyelash at this new persona his friend had taken on.

"Please join the other guests in the kitchen," Shaun said. "May I offer you a beverage?"

Darcy stared in awe at Shaun's large, modern house, with its plate glass windows, meticulous Asian landscaping and backyard infinity pool. "Wow, this is where you live? Some crash pad!"

Shaun kept up his British accent, for the moment. "Yes, we rather like it for the time being, until the renovations on the big house are completed."

"There's a bigger house?" Darcy asked.

"He's kidding," Irene said. "Shaun, drop the butler bit."

"Whatever you say, my lady."

"Now."

"Okay, Rini, okay." He whispered to Haley, "Milady's a bit peeved about my fraternizing with the guests."

Haley had noticed that a power shift had

gradually taken place between Irene and Shaun. They'd started out with Irene more or less retreating to the background because Shaun's flamboyant personality grabbed most of the attention. But as time went on, Shaun had become so attached to Irene that she began to take it for granted. Now she could say just about anything to him and he'd obey, still completely crazy about her.

This dynamic seemed to work for the couple, but Haley would hate to see Devon being bossed around by Darcy that way. It just wouldn't seem right.

In the kitchen, Irene heated milk for hot cocoa as Darcy ran her hand along the smooth marble countertop. "Everything in here just looks so . . . expensive," she cooed, her eyes on Shaun, who looked away sheepishly. Haley thought she'd never seen the unembarrassable Shaun look so uncomfortable. You'd never know by the sight of him, but yes, Shaun's parents were well-off. Very well-off. The trouble was, most of his friends weren't. Shaun didn't care; he didn't have a materialistic bone in his body and dashed headlong through life, always looking for fun, not dollar bills.

But apparently Darcy did care. She and Devon were neighbors in the Floods, the "wrong side of the tracks" in this basically affluent suburban town. Devon had turned his lack of means into a persona, outfitting himself from the thrift store where he worked and reveling in retro-seventies chic. But from the way Darcy was drooling over Shaun's luxurious house—and then, suddenly, Shaun himself—she was clearly looking to move into fancier precincts.

Irene poured the steaming milk into mugs and mixed in the powdered cocoa while Shaun took a bag of marshmallows from a cupboard. "I like my cocoa to be half marshmallow, half coconut," he said, pouring half a bag of coconut flakes into his cocoa. "Who's with me?"

"I'll stick with just the 'mallows. Toss me a couple of those, bro," Devon said. Shaun shot two marshmallows at him. Devon caught the second one in his mouth.

"I'll try it your way," Darcy said suggestively, leaning across the counter so that her boobs were bobbing in Shaun's direction. She reached out her arm and dipped a finger into Shaun's coconut-cocoa, lifted it up to her mouth and then gave it a good long lick. "Yummy."

"Rini, I don't know about you, but I think I'm suddenly in the mood for cider," Shaun said, dumping the contents of his mug down the drain. "Wanna help me retrieve some from the cellar?"

Irene whispered harshly to Haley, "You've got to do something about her. Now." And then Irene and Shaun headed downstairs.

"Is all that property out there Shaun's?" Darcy asked Haley, staring out the floor-to-ceiling windows onto the rolling lawn bordered by tall old trees. "How many acres does he have?"

"I wouldn't know," Haley answered truthfully.

"Do you think he'd mind if I had a look around for a minute?"

"Go ahead," Haley said, relieved to see Darcy disappear down the hall. She couldn't remember the last time she'd had a private moment alone with Devon. "So, how did you guys like the movie the other night? You left so quickly, we didn't get a chance to talk about it."

"What do you mean? You were the one who dashed out."

"Um, no."

"But Darcy said you were catching a ride with a neighbor," Devon replied, looking confused. "I just assumed she meant Reese."

That little skank! Haley thought, outraged that she'd been outmaneuvered by Darcy for the umpteenth time. She wouldn't let that happen again, that was for sure. "Reese? Not a chance. I haven't seen him in weeks, and the last time I did see him, he was cradling a swimsuit model on his lap in Nevis. Or didn't you see the text messages that bounced around over break?"

"So you're not—"

"Not even close. Wherever did you get that idea?"

"Well, Darcy said you two were—"

"I didn't realize Darcy was an expert on my social life. Remind me to ask her later what I'm doing for my birthday." Devon smiled and moved a little closer to Haley.

"So, the movie. I thought the cinematography was incredible," he said. "The way Korsikov played with light and shadow to emphasize the gray areas between good and evil . . ."

"Exactly," Haley said. "Especially given the title, *Days of the Sun, Nights of the Moon* . . ."

"The moonlight is a reflection of the sun," Devon said. "I got that too! It's like, some of the goodness of day spills over into night, to save the people of the village from being completely overwhelmed by evil."

"And Tatiana Morakova was so beautiful," Haley said breathlessly.

"Did you see her in *Sad Little Liudochka*?" Devon continued. "Where she becomes a heroin addict and then a prostitute, and soon she's so far gone that even when this artist who loves her tries to save her she can't be saved? It was so touching."

"I saw *Liudochka* last year," Haley said, locking eyes with Devon. Haley's father wanted her to have a good film education, and made sure she kept up on the classics and all the latest foreign films. "By the end, it was so bleak I could hardly watch it." Haley felt her eyes well up a bit.

Devon grabbed her hand and squeezed.

"What are you two talking about?" Darcy said, suddenly breezing back into the kitchen. Haley instinctively pulled her hand away, then wished she hadn't. Devon looked hurt.

"Just the movie the other night," he said lightly.

"Not that again. Yawn." Darcy dipped a cinnamon stick into Devon's hot cocoa and began sucking it like a lollipop.

"Excuse me, I think I need to hit the boys' room," Devon said, ducking out of the kitchen.

Then Irene and Shaun reappeared carrying a jug of cider. "Now, for the gingerbread," Shaun said, setting the jug down and spinning on his heel to head toward the pantry.

"Let me help you," Darcy volunteered. Irene's hair stood on end—Haley could feel the static electricity from across the counter.

"Oh no she didn't," Irene said, moving closer to the pantry to keep Shaun and Darcy within earshot. Haley joined her.

"This pantry is, like, the size of my whole house," Darcy was saying. "You know, Shaun, I never realized what a cool guy you are. You're such an individual, you know? I can tell you're a real artist because you have that artist personality. Nobody tells you what to do or how to live."

"I guess," Shaun said mechanically.

"So what do you feel like doing now, Shaunessy?" Darcy said in a seductive voice.

"Oh, she's going down," Irene whispered.

"Don't worry," Haley said. "Shaun can handle her."

"I feel like eating gingerbread and sipping on some cider," Shaun said, grabbing what he had come for and exiting the pantry as Irene and Haley hustled back to the kitchen counter. Before Devon returned from his bathroom break, Irene yanked the ponytail holder out of Haley's hair and fluffed up her shiny auburn mane.

"This is all-out war," she advised. "I wouldn't normally advocate such extreme measures, but you need to use everything you've got to defeat that little prostitot," Irene said. "We've got work to do."

• • •

Darcy may have shown her true colors at the movies, but now she's really bared her teeth. Her lack of brain-power would be fine if she were at least a nice person, but that's clearly not the case. Is she really so impressed by wealth that she'd try to steal Shaun from Irene? Those methods tend to work only in the high-powered Coco scene. Fortunately, that's not the way this crowd rolls.

If you want to take Irene up on her offer to win

Devon's heart by force, turn to page 129, AMERICAN GOTH.

But does Haley really want to continue chasing after Devon? Anyone who could be caught in Darcy's web is clearly not as gifted and talented as Haley first thought. Not that she isn't fond of the arty trio of Irene, Shaun and Devon, but the addition of Darcy sucks the air out of any room. People tend to get extremely tense whenever she's around, and lately she's always around. Maybe Devon just isn't worth the trouble. There are, after all, other fish in the sea—like, for instance, Reese Highland. To take him back, no questions asked, after his scandalous trip to Nevis, turn to page 150, RAPID RECONCILIATION.

There's also the supercute and supersmart Alex Martin. He's always had a thing for Haley. Devon might be the cooler catch, but maybe it's time Haley stopped fighting the tide and went with the flow. If you think Haley has had it with Devon and Co. now that Darcy Downer is a staple playmate, and wants to turn her attention to the future, turn to page 135, COLLEGE BOUND.

Meanwhile, school's been back in session for a mere week and Principal Crum is already on the warpath. He's been heard around the halls of Hillsdale High muttering the words "scandalous" and "frightening." Haley doesn't know what it's all about, but it sure seems as though something big is up. If you'd rather discover why

Hillsdale is currently on high alert, turn to page 142, PRINCIPAL CRUM'S LITANY.

There are a lot of paths Haley could take at this point, and they all lead down wildly different roads. Luckily, you're the one in the driver's seat.

DRIVING PRACTICE

Even a mall parking lot can be the scene of a crash.

"Are you sure you don't mind this, Annie?" Haley asked for the tenth time. She sat nervously behind the wheel of Annie's brand-new electric car, with Annie riding shotgun and Dave and Alex in the backseat. Dave had a notebook in his lap and a pen at the ready to write down every mistake Haley made, since Annie had offered to let Haley use her car to practice for her driving test. Dave was pretending to be the Department of Motor Vehicles road tester so that Haley wouldn't be so nervous when she faced the real thing. And Alex, he was busily doing a seating chart for the upcoming inauguration dinner.

Haley was impressed he'd come along for the ride, actually. Alex kept saying how busy he was at his internship with the governor-elect, but then, at every chance he got, he seemed to find a way to be around Haley, even if it meant lugging his work with him and staying up a little later at night.

Haley already had her learner's permit, which allowed her to practice driving with an adult over twenty-one. There currently was not an adult over twenty-one in the car. What she was about to do was totally illegal, and she knew it. But she wasn't driving on the open road, just in the mall parking lot, so she told herself it was okay. Besides, her parents had been too busy to practice with her, and she needed practice desperately. If this was the only way to get it, what other choice did she have?

She was, however, surprised that Alex hadn't objected. He was hoping for a political career of his own someday, and getting arrested by a mall Pinkerton for letting a permit driver take the wheel wouldn't exactly be a boon for his résumé.

"Sure I'm sure," Annie said. "What could happen in a parking lot? Put the car in drive and let's do a slow circle around the mall."

Dave leaned over the front seat to watch as Haley shifted the car into drive and gingerly stepped on the gas.

"Dave, do you mind?" she said. "You're making me nervous."

"How do you think you'll feel when it's not us watching you but some fat, chain-smoking DMV drone with body odor?" Dave asked.

Haley rolled her eyes. "Just sit back a little, please." She started slowly around the lot, turning carefully.

"Good," Annie said. "You're doing great."

"This isn't so hard," Haley said.

"This is the easy part," Annie said.

Haley made it all the way around the lot without incident. "Great," Annie said. "Now let's practice vertical parking. Pull over to that empty area over there." She pointed to a far corner of the parking lot where hardly any cars were parked.

"Aye, aye, cap'n." Haley felt her confidence growing. She drove slowly down a crowded row of parked cars toward the desolate corner of the lot.

Suddenly a black SUV backed out of a spot right in front of her. "Brake, brake!" Annie yelled. Haley slammed on the brakes just in time. Everyone in the car bolted forward, restrained by their seat belts. Haley had missed the SUV by a hair. The driver mouthed angry words at her through the closed window of his fortresslike vehicle.

Haley sat frozen.

"Back up, Haley!" Annie yelled. "Before the guy plows right over us!"

Haley snapped herself out of her trance and put the car into reverse. She looked around in every direction for telltale red taillights—nobody backing out that she could see—before tentatively touching the gas pedal. The SUV jerked the rest of the way out of its spot and roared off. Haley put the car into park and tried to catch her breath.

Annie undid her seat belt. "Okay, Evel Knievel. I think that's enough for today." She jumped out and ran over to open the driver's-side door. Still in a daze and on the verge of tears, Haley got out of the car and returned to the passenger seat, her driving lesson over almost as quickly as it had begun.

"That was close, too close," Dave said, a nervous shake in his voice. "Why did I get into a car with a student driver? I'm an idiot!"

"Calm down, you guys," Alex said. "There was no harm done. And that actually wasn't Haley's fault. The driver of the SUV should have looked before pulling out in front of us like that."

"I had the right-of-way," Haley said. "Didn't I?"

"That's my point," Alex said.

"But Haley didn't react fast enough," Annie said. "That's what matters when you're driving on the road for real." She lovingly patted the dashboard. "My beautiful little car almost got smashed by that monster SUV!"

"I'm really sorry, Annie," Haley said. "To all of you."

"You definitely do need practice, that's obvious," Annie said.

Haley was inclined to agree. She was hoping to get her license on her birthday and not a day later, since her parents had hinted that she might find a car waiting for her in the driveway. If that little wish came true, she wanted to be able to drive the car immediately—without her parents riding shotgun. "From now on, if you want a practice car, use your boyfriend Alex's," Annie added.

"Boyfriend?" Haley shot Annie a baffled, annoyed look. Why did Annie have to use that word? Annie raised her eyebrows high over her eyeglass frames as if to say, *Well, that's what he is, isn't he?*

Haley glanced at Alex and could see immediately that he'd caught the look that had passed between the girls. *Oh God,* she thought. *Things are going to be awkward between us now. If only Annie hadn't used the b word. . . .*

"Well, my girlfriend can practice in my car anytime she wants," he said lightly. "That's what boyfriends are for, right?"

Haley tried to laugh along with him. It was gentlemanly of him to make a joke out of the awkward situation Annie had created.

"Thanks." Haley admired how calm he was in the face of a near accident. He'd probably make a great driving tutor, she thought. That is, if Annie didn't scare him away first.

• • •

Things are warming up fast between Haley and Alex—at least it looks that way to Haley. There's always room for misinterpretation, but Haley's got a good feeling about this. Of course, the closer she gets to a love connection with Alex, the harder it will be to back out. So she'd better be sure she wants to pursue this or there could be hurt feelings all around.

If you're sure Haley wants to explore the possibilities with Alex, turn to page 135, COLLEGE BOUND. If you think she should take her time to see what other opportunities arise and find out the latest buzz at Hillsdale High, turn to page 142, PRINCIPAL CRUM'S LITANY.

INAUGURATION

There's nothing sexier to a policy wonk than . . . politics.

"You're stunning," Alex said, helping Haley into the passenger seat of his father's European sedan.

"You're late," she said, smiling.

Alex winced. "Mrs. Eton needed some last-minute help with her speech," he said, seeming genuinely contrite. Then he broke into a huge grin. "How is anyone going to look at the governor once you walk into the room?"

"Think you can get off that easily?"

"Have I mentioned you look stunning?"

"Twice."

Haley had borrowed the dress she was wearing, a vintage strapless number that was black and beaded and shaped like a mermaid, from her mother. It had been sitting in Joan's closet since Joan and Perry's ten-year college reunion, and from the minute Haley put it on, she looked far older than her almost-seventeen years. In fact, her father nearly didn't let her out of the house. Luckily, Joan had convinced him to let Haley go—even if the party was to celebrate a Republican reaching high office.

Alex drove carefully the whole way, as if he were carrying precious cargo, and every few minutes he turned to look at Haley and smile. When they were almost to Princeton, he said, "I can say with all honesty, Haley, that tonight is the absolute best night of my life."

"But Alex, we haven't even gotten to the party yet!"

"I know, I just didn't want to forget to say it."

Alex stopped his car in front of Drumthwacket, the governor's executive mansion, and waited as the valets hurried over to open their doors for them.

"You know, you don't look so bad yourself," Haley said as Alex took her arm to escort her inside.

It was true: she'd never seen Alex look so handsome. His tuxedo fit him perfectly and his eyes had a twinkle in them that lit up his face. Haley didn't know if that twinkle came from his love of politics or from being with her, but it didn't matter—either way, the inaugural ball was turning out to be a dream date so far.

When Alex had first invited her to the inauguration, it felt natural to accept—and that made Haley suddenly giddy that things were getting more serious between them, like way more serious. Which was a good thing, as far as she was concerned. She liked the way she felt around Alex: secure, natural, able to let her hair down without worrying what he would think of her.

After seeing what some of the other junior girls at school were going through with their boyfriends, she realized what a gift it was to be able to be herself around a guy and not worry the least little bit about him straying. Coco, Sasha and Cecily, on the other hand, seemed to be on a drama binge, having dumped their boyfriends and undertaken drastic diets and makeovers to make the boys feel the loss even more keenly. But what was the point of all that effort? If you had to bend over backward to make a boy like you, was he even worth it in the end?

Alex was a senior and so much more mature than Drew, Johnny, Spencer or even Reese Highland, boys who were only one year younger but suddenly seemed like children. Being with Alex felt like being with a college guy. He was calm, smart and sensible. He had lofty, admirable goals and he treated Haley as if she were just as mature as he was. She loved it.

They stopped at the threshold of the ballroom and surveyed the scene. They had played a large part in planning the party, after all, especially Alex. The room looked beautiful and so far everything seemed to be running smoothly. Alex turned to her and said, "Ready to go knock their socks off?"

She beamed at him. "Ready."

"First, let's go congratulate Mrs. Eton," Alex said. Haley followed him across the dance floor to a knot of people near the bar. The group parted, revealing Mrs. Eton at the center. She was dressed like a queen in a silver gown trimmed with white fur; her diamond earrings were massive.

A young man, clearly one of Mrs. Eton's aides, spoke first. "Hey, Alex, nice legwork. Everything looks great."

"Oh, Alex, there you are." Mrs. Eton reached out to shake his hand. "In case any of you don't know Alex Martin, this is one of my bright young interns. He has a very promising future in politics, I assure you. We're very lucky to have him on the Republican side, and I intend to keep him there!"

There was laughter, and a few members of the crowd—reporters, Haley guessed—jotted down notes. One woman asked Alex how to spell his name. Haley felt proud to be with him; he was so obviously respected by everyone he worked with, even though he was only eighteen.

"Governor Eton, I'd like you to meet Haley Miller," Alex said, stepping aside to make room for Haley.

She held out her hand and the governor shook it. "Lovely to see you, Haley."

"It's an honor to be here," Haley said. "Congratulations, and best of luck in your new job."

"Thank you, dear. I'm going to need it." Mrs. Eton grinned and turned to one of the reporters. "If you have any more questions, get them over with, please. I'd like to celebrate!"

The entourage laughed as if this were the wittiest remark they'd ever heard. Haley followed Alex to their table to set down her evening bag, snagging a glass of sparkling water from a passing tray.

"Haley? Is that you?" A tall woman Haley's mother's age stopped her and smiled. It was Karen Warshaw, a state senator who'd fought alongside Joan Miller to stop the opening of a mill that would pollute the Delaware River. "I almost didn't recognize you, you look so grown up."

"Hello, Karen," Haley said. "This is Alex Martin. He's an intern with Governor Eton. Alex, this is Karen Warshaw, state senator."

"Senator, Haley's told me wonderful things about your work on education reform," Alex said, shaking her hand. "It's a pleasure to meet you. You know, I share your support for charter schools and inventive solutions in teacher training. The unions have grown too big and powerful. It's time to restore checks and balances."

"What a charming young man," Karen said in a low voice to Haley. "But does your mother know you've crossed enemy lines?"

They all laughed. Inauguration Day was a celebration of democracy, Haley thought, a time to take off the gloves and put politics aside, if only for a day.

"Please give your mother my best," Karen said, walking off. "And tell her I think I'll have another case for her soon."

"Thanks for saving me there," Alex said. "I should know her name but I drew a total blank. She's one of the governor's fiercest critics—and Mrs. Eton likes to keep her enemies close."

"You're welcome. Here comes Eli Morgenstern. Remember, his wife's a Democrat and it embarrasses him, so don't bring up anything too partisan."

"Gotcha. Mr. and Mrs. Morgenstern, hello!" Mr. Morgenstern was a wealthy investor in his seventies who was a major contributor to the Republican Party. Nobody in politics could afford to get on his bad side. He looked very at home in a tuxedo, probably from years of attending charity events. His wife, twenty years younger, shone in a gold Japanese kimono dress.

Alex and Haley had a pleasant five-minute

conversation with the Morgensterns about Mrs. Morgenstern's passion, Japanese art. By the end, the older couple were exclaiming over the well-mannered, nice young couple who knew so much about so many different subjects.

"Whew," Alex said to Haley. "I'd hate to offend that guy. The governor would never forgive me."

"You've got nothing to worry about," Haley said. "They loved you."

"Correction: they loved us," Alex said.

For the rest of the cocktail hour and all through dinner, Alex and Haley worked as a team. Haley conversed easily with people of all stripes, most of whom were years older than she was. The challenging family dinner conversations she'd grown up with were paying off. When Alex's memory occasionally failed him under pressure, Haley effortlessly filled in the blanks, reminding him of names and occupations. Thanks to her mother's political work, Haley knew more people at the ball than she expected—and they knew her. By the time dinner broke up for dancing, Alex was very impressed with his date.

"You should go into politics," he said, leading Haley onto the dance floor. "You're very good with people."

"Thanks," Haley said, "but I'm not sure politics is my thing."

"I'm telling you, you're a natural," Alex said.

They danced to the swing band until they got thirsty and headed back to the bar. Mrs. Eton was sitting nearby, talking to the Morgensterns.

"We're having a wonderful time, Eleanor," Mrs. Morgenstern was saying. "I don't remember the last time we went to a political function without ending up in a terrible argument."

"Not tonight, though," Mr. Morgenstern said. "I vowed we wouldn't fight tonight." He waved Alex and Haley over. "Here's that cute young couple, the future of America. I'd just about given up on this generation until I met these two."

"That's my intern," Governor Eton said proudly. "I hired him myself. He's from good Republican stock, and it shows. He's got the smarts and great work ethic to prove it."

Mrs. Morgenstern blanched, and Haley saw trouble coming. "Governor Eton, are you suggesting that brains and hard work are exclusive traits of the Republican Party?" Mrs. Morgenstern said, in high dudgeon.

"Diana, don't start," Mr. Morgenstern snapped.

"Of course not," Mrs. Eton said, eyeing Haley. "After all, Haley here is a Democrat." The governor then gave a conspiratorial wink to Alex, as in, *Your lefty date just saved my butt!*

"The real issue for young people is not which party they belong to, but getting them involved at all," Haley said, deftly shifting the conversation.

"Did you know voter registration among eighteen-year-olds is only thirty percent?"

Mrs. Eton nodded, recognizing political expediency when she saw it. "She's absolutely right, of course. We must get more young people involved, no matter what party they choose. There are many Democrats whom I admire and trust, Diana, and I count you among them."

"Thank you, Eleanor," Mrs. Morgenstern said. "That's very gracious of you."

"Crisis averted," Alex whispered to Haley. "Quick thinking, H."

They turned to find themselves face to face with Spencer Eton, Mrs. Eton's dissolute son. His face looked puffy and bleary and he reeked of alcohol. *What a way to behave at your mother's inauguration,* Haley thought. *Mrs. E. is not going to like this one bit.*

"Hey, Spencer," Alex said. "Haven't seen you all night. Where's Coco?"

Haley elbowed Alex but it was too late. Spencer scowled. "'Where's Coco? Where's Coco?' How come everybody keeps asking about Coco? You'd think they'd rather see her here than me."

Haley glanced back at Mrs. Eton, who'd clearly overheard the conversation. Mrs. Eton rose to her feet and glided over to join them. "Are you still mooning?" she said to Spencer. "This breakup has caused entirely too much trouble in this family at the worst possible moment. Could that girl not have waited another week? Spencer, darling, you're better off without her, believe me."

"No girl has ever broken up with me," Spencer said, to no one in particular. "And have you seen her lately? She looks better than she did when we were dating."

"Oh, enough about her," Mrs. Eton said. "If only . . ." She turned to Alex and pulled him aside. "Young man, I've got a very important job for you. Ever since that girl broke up with my son, he's been a wreck. The whole episode has hurt his self-image. He needs to be back on top. You go to school with them. Isn't there something you could do?"

"But Mrs. Eton," Alex protested, "I don't think I have the power to—"

"You'll find a way because you have to, Alex," Mrs. Eton said. "Trust me. This is your first real lesson in politics—and real politics is cutthroat politics. It's what goes on behind the scenes, not what the public sees. Do I have your word?"

"Um," Alex said, "I'm sure I can think of something."

Spencer continued to sulk in the corner. Mrs. Eton patted him on the cheek and walked away. Haley stared after her, stunned. Was this how New Jersey's taxpayers' money would be spent—helping restore Spencer Eton's social status?

• • •

Haley has made a wonderful impression on a lot of important people tonight. Is she cut out for politics, as Alex said? Or is her flirtation with state power just a one-night fling?

If you think the inauguration has been an exciting evening for Haley, and one that will lead to a great future for her, turn to page 135, COLLEGE BOUND. If you think the political system at high school is far more entertaining than talking issues with a bunch of suits, see what the lead-tongued leader of Hillsdale High has to say on page 142, PRINCIPAL CRUM'S LITANY.

Finally, if you don't like the way Mrs. Eton is meddling in her son's private life—and dragging Alex into it by employing him to get Spencer back on top—side with Team Coco on page 153, STICK WITH THE SISTERHOOD.

MAN DOWN

Breaking hearts doesn't come easily to everyone.

"This is it, girls," Coco commanded. "D-day. Everyone into formation."

Haley, Sasha and Cecily lined up beside Coco in a fighter-pilot V formation and prepared to march through Hillsdale High on their search-and-destroy-relationships mission. Coco had made sure they all looked their hottest for maximum impact. She had personally supervised Haley's makeup application by Whitney at the health club that morning and loaned her a miniskirt, saying that the slim knee-length dress Haley had originally chosen was too conservative.

"We need to make their eyeballs pop out," Coco reminded the girls. They were a team of gleaming, shiny-haired, toned, lip-glossed beauties by the time they stepped into the breezeway, their smoking looks matched only by their appetite for destruction.

The sea of students parted as the girls marched through the crowd. "There's Drew," Coco said, homing in on the cute football star. "Go, Cecily."

Cecily peeled off from the group and pinned Drew against the wall as the rest of the girls walked past without breaking stride. Haley glanced back and caught a glimpse of Drew's horrified face as Cecily broke the news: they were splitsville.

"One down," Coco said triumphantly. "Three to go."

Sasha saw Johnny Lane headed for his locker and veered out of formation to nab him there. Again Haley couldn't resist glancing back. Sasha was coldly dumping Johnny as—shock of shocks—he actually started tearing up. He tried to pull Sasha into a hug but she ruthlessly pushed him away, turned her back and walked off. The carnage the girls were leaving in their wake was impressive, Haley thought.

"Come on, Haley, don't slow down now," Coco barked. "No second thoughts. We all agreed, and this is what's best for everybody. For those of us with two X chromosomes anyway. Now march!"

Left, right, left, right . . . Big target up ahead: Spencer Eton.

"This one's mine," Coco muttered. She flew at him like a bee going in for the killer sting. His smile faded fast when he saw her expression and turned to utter shock when she slapped him right across the face.

Good old Coco, Haley thought. *Gets right to the point.*

The first three victims went down hard. Haley started feeling a little nervous as her target, Reese, loomed up ahead. Her mind suddenly emptied. What would she say to him? What did Coco tell her to say? She couldn't remember.

Reese's face lit up when he saw her. That threw her. Instead of going in for the kill, Haley stopped dead in her tracks. Could she really go through with this?

You have to, she told herself. *All the other girls did. They're counting on you.*

"Haley!" Reese said happily. He hurtled toward her, threw his arms around her and enveloped her in a bear hug. Her muscles, so tense just a second earlier, warmed and relaxed at his touch.

"I'm so glad to see you! I missed you so much."

He pulled back and gazed at her face with real affection. She felt more confused than ever.

"Is something wrong?" he asked, ever sensitive and able to read her. "Listen, I know some rumors have been going around about what happened in Nevis. I've been trying to talk to you about it but you never returned my calls!"

"I know," Haley said.

"I've got to tell you what happened," he said. "I know you'll believe me." Haley braced herself for whatever was coming—but it turned out to be not as bad as she expected.

Speak, Haley told herself. *Say something. Now's the time when you break the news to him: he's officially dumped.*

But the words wouldn't come. She felt conflicted, and then there was his adorable smile tugging at her heart. . . . Her stupid heart, definitely her weak spot. Why couldn't she be cold and strong like the other girls? But they had it easy. They only had to dump ordinary boys. They didn't have to try to resist someone as special as Reese. He was so good-looking, so charming, and when he spoke of how he missed her he seemed so sincere. . . .

No, she thought, *it's a trap. He knows exactly what he's doing. I've got to speak up. . . .*

But before she had a chance to say a word, he leaned in to kiss her. This was her last chance. She could kiss him back . . . or turn away for good.

• • •

Haley needs to get up the nerve to act, pronto, or else abort the mission. If she can't pull the trigger on Reese, if she doesn't have the nerve to go through with their D-day plans, what will the other girls think? After they broke the hearts of Drew, Spencer and Johnny, what will they say if Haley wimps out?

On the other hand . . . it's Reese. He's always been different, not just one of the guys. Maybe he does have a good explanation for why he was photographed with a hot girl on his lap. Haley has always thought of Reese as a fine, upstanding citizen—too upstanding, sometimes—and generally a good, honest guy. He brought up Nevis before she even had a chance to say anything. Doesn't that point to his innocence? Or does it point to his cunning—trying to dismiss the subject before Haley even had a chance to call him on it, and then using his physical magnetism to push aside her fears?

If you think Haley is only human after all and that she can't resist the temptation of Reese's pillow-soft lips, have her enter into a RAPID RECONCILIATION with him on page 150. If you think there is no way Haley is going to be the only one to let down the girls and break their sisterhood pact, STICK WITH THE SISTERHOOD on page 153. Finally, if you think Haley wishes she could snap her fingers and make all her boy problems disappear, head to page 142, PRINCIPAL CRUM'S

LITANY, to distract her with issues that might be bigger than her own.

Reese's kisser is headed straight for Haley's. She can either turn her head or meet him halfway. It's up to you.

ON THE SCALE

The holidays can weigh heavily on a girl.

Haley went into her mother's bathroom and stared at the vintage doctor's scale next to the sink. Joan Miller had scored the scale at an antique show back in California. Haley hadn't weighed herself in a while; she usually didn't feel the need to. But all this talk lately about models and bikinis and diets had made her think it might be time to check on her poundage.

She stepped onto the scale and moved the lead weights to the usual numbers. Her eyes widened as the arrow clanked heavily upward. Apparently she put on a few pounds.

Or maybe not, she thought, glancing down at her jeans and heavy winter sweater. Maybe it was just her clothes that had gotten heavier. She took everything off and stepped onto the scale again. That was a little better, but not much. Haley couldn't believe her eyes. Could that number really be right?

It's an old scale, she told herself. *It could be out of whack.*

But her mother weighed herself on this scale every day, and seemed to trust it. Haley decided to give it one more chance.

She exhaled and stepped on one more time. The arrow balanced in the same place as before: no change. She couldn't kid herself anymore: she weighed more than she ever had in her life.

Okay, so I put on a few pounds, Haley told herself. *I'm a growing girl.* After a holiday filled with sweet treats—not in the Miller house, of course, but at various holiday parties around town—and a few too many Golden Dynasty dinners, who wouldn't gain a little weight?

She looked at herself in the full-length mirror and pinched a bit of skin at her waistline. She had to face facts. The weight gain was nothing a woolly winter sweater couldn't hide, but she had to admit she wasn't at her ideal fighting weight. But did it really matter? And if so, what should she do about it?

• • •

[illegible] Haley feels insecure after her breakup with [illegible] that gaining weight is the last thing she wants to deal with, take it to the extreme and have her try to shed ten pounds superfast on page 162, SLIMMING EFFECT.

If you think that after spending the holidays surrounded by cakes, cookies and holiday meals (even tofu is fattening if you put sesame sauce on it), Haley will feel better if she goes on a health kick, turn to page 153, STICK WITH THE SISTERHOOD. If you think Haley figures it's winter so who cares anyway, make her keep up her Golden Dynasty habits on page 127, AMERICAN GOTH. To have Haley continue her normal, mostly healthy habits because you think she looks great the way she is, even with a little winter padding to keep her warm, turn to page 135, COLLEGE BOUND. Finally, if you think Haley Miller doesn't have body image issues but the other girls at her school do, listen to PRINCIPAL CRUM'S LITANY on page 142.

The weight issue is practically a rite of passage for teenaged girls. How Haley handles it could affect everything from her social life to her health, so don't take her down the wrong path, or she could lose more than weight—namely, everything she holds dear.

IV

If you starve your body, your brain weakens too.

Haley slowly peeled a single segment from the orange on her lap. She put it into her mouth and savored it, letting the fruit dissolve, noting every nuance of the flavor. It was a pleasant sensation at first, but then her stomach seized on the first drop of juice, snarling and growling and practically tearing itself apart. This was the part that didn't feel great, but then, beauty was worth a little pain, right?

Haley had decided to go all out and follow the Coco Cleanse to the letter, in the hopes that a new year and a newly svelte her would punish Reese Highland for his flirtatious hijinks with a swimsuit model in Nevis. For the first few days, Coco had instructed her to consume only hot water and lemon juice. Now they were on to green tea and oranges. And so far she was doing great, if not quite feeling that way. Haley had made it through five days and had shed almost as many pounds. Her goal of ten pounds in ten days was now within sight. And she'd also been able to break herself of her early habit of drinking gallons of water to mask her hunger. "That only adds water weight," Coco had said disapprovingly.

At school, it was easy to do the cleanse. Nobody watched what Haley ate for lunch, and she had Coco, Sasha, Whitney and Cecily for support. They were all doing the cleanse too, and the fad quickly spread to other girls in their class.

At home it was trickier. Her parents expected her to eat dinner, but even brown rice and vegetables were too fattening for Coco's extreme regimen. So Haley usually just told Joan and Perry she was eating at Coco's house—Coco's parents were hardly ever around, and they never had any inkling what their daughter was up to. If she didn't go to Coco's, she stayed late at the library and came home after dinner hour, telling her mother she'd already eaten.

All her tactics seemed to be working. The only hard part was continuing not to eat. She had gradually gotten used to the acid buildup—with nothing to digest, her stomach was trying to eat itself—and the intense cravings for simple carbs like plain pasta or milk to coat her rumbling stomach. But she held firm, and was often so light-headed from lack of protein she barely even noticed the pain in her abdomen between "meals." The dizziness was slightly alarming, but her cheekbones had grown so prominent Haley hardly even cared. Besides, Coco and the other girls kept cheering her on. It was kind of like a contest—who can eat the least? Who's the most virtuous dieter?—and Haley wasn't about to lose.

That was before she had to go through an hour-long gym class. Haley had found herself too tired to finish ten sit-ups. That wasn't like her at all—usually she could do fifty easily—and the gym teacher of course took notice. "Aren't you feeling well, Haley?" Ms. Wissman asked, staring at the dark circles under Haley's eyes and the sallow look of her skin. "Maybe you should sit today out."

"Thanks," Haley said. She'd wanted to do more sit-ups—nothing better for toning the abs—but it felt good to sit on the bleachers and rest for a minute. The other girls stared at her enviously, wishing they could get out of gym too. *I bet they wish they had as much self-control as I have,* Haley thought. *I bet they wish they could live on oranges and tea and get super skinny.* But then she started feeling dizzy again and had to lie down on the bleacher bench.

By her afternoon history class, she could barely concentrate; all she wanted to do was rest her head on her desk. When someone said something to her, she was slow to respond. And Shaun Willkommen asked her if she'd turned into an alien because her skin looked so green. Finally her history teacher, Mr. Tygert, sent her to the nurse's office. The dreaded Ms. Underhill—Haley had been hoping to avoid her, but now she had no choice.

"What seems to be the trouble?" stocky Ms. Underhill asked, taking Haley's vital signs.

"Nothing," Haley insisted. "I'm just a little tired, that's all."

"You look exhausted," the nurse said, shifting her considerable weight from one foot to the other. She examined Haley with an expression of concern. "And if I'm not mistaken, you are seriously dehydrated, my dear. How did you get yourself in this terrible shape? You need to be put on IV fluids immediately. Here, let's get you onto a gurney."

"I'll just drink a little water," Haley said, trying to stand up. Her knees buckled and when she came to, her head ached, she felt nauseated and there was a strange, wet, metallic taste in her mouth: blood.

"Haley? Haley? Are you all right?" Nurse Underhill was saying.

"What happened?"

"You tried to get up and walk out of here, and you passed out and smacked your face on the edge of the gurney. Here, let me get a bandage on that cheek. You're going to have one massive shiner there, young lady. And I'll be surprised if that cut doesn't leave a scar."

Ms. Underhill helped Haley up to the bed in her office. "Now, let's get some fluids into you, or you're going to end up in the hospital." She loaded up an IV and jabbed it into Haley's arm. Then she checked her computer for Haley's "in case of emergency" contacts. "Is your mother at work today? If she can't come right away, I may have to call an ambulance. Dehydration is extremely serious. You could damage your kidneys, have liver failure or heart trouble. . . ."

"Please don't call my mother," Haley begged.

"What, you think I can just let you leave with a bag of fluids hooked up to your arm?" Nurse Underhill replied.

"Nurse Underhill, do IV fluids have calories?" Haley asked. "Coco is going to be so pissed."

Ms. Underhill's tough face hardened. "Haley Miller, don't tell me you're on this so-called diet cleanse? I thought you were smarter than that!"

Haley hung her head.

"That diet is running rampant through this school," Ms. Underhill said. "You're the third girl I've seen this week with eating problems. It's growing to epidemic proportions." She dialed Haley's mother's work number. "Mrs. Miller? This is Nurse Underhill at Hillsdale High. No, I'm afraid everything is not okay. I've got Haley here and she's seriously dehydrated. Yes, I don't think she's had anything to eat in several days. No, she's put herself on a cleanse diet, and she almost put herself in the emergency room. No, of course, I'll make sure she stays right here until you arrive."

Haley felt herself losing consciousness again. She shut her eyes and wished she could go back in time five days and change everything. She hurt all over, but what hurt the most was knowing she'd brought all this pain on herself—and the thought of what her parents would say when they got ahold of her.

● ● ●

Who would have thought five days of starving yourself could cause so much damage? Your foolish choices have brought on dire consequences for Haley. Not only will she not end up model-thin, but now her face is disfigured, maybe permanently. Hang your head and go **back to page 1.**

DEAD END

You can turn a girl into a punk but you can't make her slam dance.

"Irene, I know you think there's still a chance for me and Devon," Haley said, plopping down on her bed, "but did you see the way they were all over each other in the parking lot today? I can only imagine what they're doing right now in the Floods. Ew."

Irene and Haley were hanging out in Haley's bedroom, trying to figure out what to do about the D-Squared problem, as they now called it. It seemed that no matter what Haley did to try to lure Devon away from his freshman siren, she only seemed to push him further into Darcy's clutches.

"That's wack and you know it," Irene said. "You're the one Dev has so much in common with. You're the one he wants to be with. He just hasn't figured it out yet. He only likes that little twit because she's hot—albeit in a trashtastic sort of way—and it doesn't take much for her to lift her skirt."

"Exactly," Haley said. "How am I supposed to get his attention when she's always on her back?"

"You've got to take one for the team here, Haley," Irene persisted. "It's getting to the point where Shaun and I can't be friends with Devon anymore unless he ditches Darcy. You're our only hope. You've got to do something to catch his attention—and keep it away from her—or . . ."

"Or what?" Haley demanded.

"Well, maybe we'll get to the point where we can't be friends with you either," Irene huffed.

What's that supposed to mean? Haley wondered, glaring at her friend. She was beginning to tire of Irene always blaming her for Devon's taste in women. "Look, I've tried practically everything. The movie was a complete disaster. He doesn't seem to care that Darcy is a total moron." Haley tried on a pair of jeans and frowned at herself in the mirror on the back of her closet door. "Wow, my jeans are getting really tight."

"So?" Irene said. "Aren't they supposed to be tight?"

"Not this tight," Haley said, struggling with the top snap. "I've gained about five pounds since Christmas. One too many Golden Dynasty egg rolls, I guess."

She studied herself in the mirror, not sure what to think of her newly plump figure. Maybe her jeans didn't fit, but she was curvier, which was good, right?

"You look fantastic," Irene said. "Better than ever. Healthier. I've always thought you were a touch on the skinny side."

"Um, easy for you to say that," Haley said. Irene was fine-boned and slender, not the least bit heavy.

"You know what? Forget jeans," Irene said, a sudden twinkle in her eye. "Jeans are dullsville. Everybody wears jeans. What you need is a brand-new look, something totally wild." She got up and went to the closet. "In fact, that could be the answer to our problem."

"What are you talking about?" Haley said.

Irene opened the closet and started pawing through Haley's clothes. "A way to get Devon's attention." She pulled out a fluffy pink cardigan with a Mrs. Claus stitched across the breast. Irene pinched the sweater between her fingers at arm's length, half frightened, half disgusted. "What the elf? Haley, tell me this is supposed to be ironic."

Haley sighed. The sweater was one of Gam Polly's knitted abominations. Every Christmas up until just last year, Haley's grandmother had given her and Mitchell something she'd knitted herself, and it was usually unwearable. "I wish," Haley said. "I have Gam Polly to thank for that."

"I can't get over some of this stuff. Penny loafers? Khakis? What were you thinking?"

"I know, I know," Haley said. "I used to give my mom too much power over my wardrobe."

"Hello . . . what's this?" Irene pulled out Haley's old gray plaid Montessori-school kilt. In California, before moving east to New Jersey, Haley had gone to a Montessori school and worn a uniform. She was surprised to find it was still in her closet. She had thought she'd never wear it again, and good riddance.

"This is perfect," Irene said. "Do you have any scissors?"

Haley grabbed some scissors off her desk and gave them to Irene, who started hacking at the plaid skirt's hemline until it was ragged and enticingly short. "Here," Irene said, tossing Haley a plastic shopping bag she'd brought over from the drugstore. "Look through there and pick out some makeup."

The bag was full of cosmetics, from burgundy lipstick to heavy black eyeliner to green hair dye. Everything a girl needed for a punk rock makeover.

Irene tossed the freshly cropped skirt and a Clash T-shirt at her. "There's your new uniform. Now let's hit the bathroom. I'll show you the way to make Devon McKnight melt."

Two hours later, Haley stepped into her room with a green streak in her messed-up auburn hair and a new punk-glam look. The chopped-off kilt stopped mid-thigh, well above her combat boots. The rip in her Clash T-shirt was held together with two large safety pins. Her eyes were practically blackened with eyeliner, her lips stained a ghoulish purple. She ran to the full-length mirror.

"You look scary," Irene said. "In a totally hot way."

"Thanks." Haley turned in front of the mirror, trying to get used to the alien person reflected back at her. It was amazing how a few cosmetic changes could transform a girl, even suggest a completely different personality. Was this what Devon wanted? Haley had to admit that her new look made her feel bolder and wilder.

Mitchell passed by Haley's door and stopped cold. "Is it Halloween? Did I forget about Halloween?"

"Mitchell, go away," Haley said.

Mitchell refused to obey. "Wait—it can't be Halloween. It's January! What happened to you? You look like you slammed face-first into a clown and he left half his makeup on you."

Haley frowned. "Very helpful. Now get out of here."

"Has Mom seen you yet?" Mitchell said. "Because when she does, you're going to be in biiiig trouble."

"I said get out of here." Haley took him by the shoulders, turned him toward the hallway and marched him out of the room, shutting the door behind him.

"Just let me be there when you show Mom!" Mitchell shouted through the door. "Please?"

"Go away," Haley said. "Ignore him," she added to Irene, though she felt a twinge of guilt. Mitchell was an odd boy who didn't have a lot of friends, and she sometimes thought he seemed lonely. Of course, if he wanted to hang around Haley, he didn't have to insult her.

"I already have," Irene said. "Now, remember what I told you: the outfit alone is not enough. The real key to this makeover is your attitude. The new look is just the outward manifestation of it. You're tough—you don't care about anything or anybody, least of all Devon McKnight. Trust me, you do this and he'll realize what a fool he's been." She smiled deviously.

"But how do you know it will work?"

"Because I know Devon," Irene said. "Think about it, the way he's jerked you around all this time. Why? Because he can never make up his mind. About anything. He acts cool but at heart he's very indecisive. Wishy-washy, even. That makes him easy pickings for a tattoo-covered scam artist like Darcy."

"Or me," Haley said, a kernel of doubt rising in her mind as she touched the green streak in her hair.

"You're not a scam artist," Irene insisted. "You're his soul mate. The girl he was meant to be with. We just have to help clue him in."

"And you think all this will convince him?"

"He'll love the new you, but remember—it's the attitude that will seal the deal," Irene said. "I hate to say anything nice about that Stepford chick Coco, but one thing I'll give her: she's been a pro at freezing out Spencer since she dumped him last week. The more he begs for forgiveness the colder she gets—and it just keeps him coming back for more. That is exactly what you need to do to Devon. And if you can keep it up, soon he'll be right where you want him: wrapped around your skull-ringed little finger."

● ● ●

Looks as though Haley's trying to outpunk her rival, Darcy. And since she and Devon actually do have more in common than Devon and Darcy, this style change might be the tipping point in Haley's conquest of the adorably arty photographer.

Every change comes with a price, however. And if Irene's clever plan doesn't work—or worse yet,

backfires—what will Haley be left with? A vat of green hair dye and a tub of humiliation? Is it worth the risk?

And what if Mitchell is right—will Joan Miller take one look at Green Day Haley and scrub the eyeliner off until her skin is raw? Maybe Haley's little bro just said that because he's desperate for attention. As the big sister, shouldn't Haley look out for him? Or will she be too busy chasing Devon?

If you think Haley loves her punky new look and wants to take on Darcy and destroy the Devon love triangle, turn to page 166, SHOWDOWN AT JACK'S. If you think Haley should ditch this Halloween-costume look and spend more quality time with her little brother, and perhaps help him get to know his fellow oddball Dave Metzger, turn to page 174, ROBOT ER.

Finally, what if Haley decides that punk rock chic isn't her vibe? If it takes pretending to be someone she's not to get Devon, then maybe Devon isn't the guy for her. If this is your take on the situation, turn to page 188, LOVE AND ROCKETS.

Punk is an attitude for sure, and not everyone can pull it off. But can Haley? That's for you to decide.

Good news for some can be bad news for others—it's all in how you look at it.

One afternoon Haley received a mysterious text from Alex: "dnr 2nite, bubbies, 7. celebr8!"

Celebrate what? Haley wondered. She had to find out, and she couldn't resist the invitation, so she texted back: "ilbt."

She walked into Bubbies Bistro at seven that night just as Annie and Dave arrived in Annie's electric car.

"Do you know what this is all about?" Haley asked Annie.

Annie shook her head. "No idea."

Alex was sitting at the round table in the back, grinning ecstatically, his face glowing. He waved his friends over and they sat down. Each place was already set with a glass of sparkling cider.

"What's the big news?" Annie asked.

"My friends, I'm glad you could join me," Alex said. "I wanted to make this announcement in person—"

"Then hurry up and make it already!" Dave said, ever the patient diplomat.

"All right," Alex said. "I found out today that I've been accepted at Georgetown. I'll be studying poli-sci there in the fall."

"That's wonderful!" Haley cried. She threw her arms around him and gave him a huge hug. She was genuinely excited for him. Getting into Georgetown had been Alex's dream for as long as she'd known him.

"Congratulations!" Annie and Dave chorused. They all toasted Alex with their sparkling cider.

"Thank you," Alex said. "I'm really grateful to have such amazingly supportive friends to share this news with. Now, let's order some food! My treat."

After they ordered dinner and began to eat, Haley felt her excitement fade somewhat. She was truly happy for Alex, but the reality suddenly struck her: he was going away to college next year. To Washington, D.C. Not that Washington was all that far away, but still . . . he'd be in college, and she'd still be a New Jersey high school girl. How could their relationship grow under those conditions?

"Mrs. Eton was really excited for me too," Alex was saying. "She even threw together a little toast for me at the office this afternoon." He paused to eat a bite of steak.

"She must be sorry to lose you," Haley said. "She obviously thinks you're a great asset to her administration."

"She wouldn't think so highly of me if it weren't for you, Haley," Alex said. "You guys should have seen Haley at the inaugural ball! She was amazing. She knew all these influential people, and she remembered everybody's name and what their interests were and who was enemies with whom. . . . She really saved my butt a few times—and Governor Eton's, too."

"Really?" Annie eyed her with suspicion. "I thought you were dreading hobnobbing with those Republicans."

Haley blushed, pleased by Alex's praise, even as the pit in her stomach grew. That night at the inaugural ball had been wonderful, but also a little unsettling. Haley had felt so competent, so on top of her game and in perfect sync with Alex—until Governor Eton had practically commanded him to take down Coco De Clerq so that Mrs. Eton's son Spencer's social status in Hillsdale would once again be restored.

Ever since then, Alex had secretly been working on undermining Coco, and Haley had been glad he hadn't asked her to get her hands dirty. Yet. As she looked over at Alex, and caught herself smiling at his handsome face, nerdy glasses and bow tie, it began to dawn on her just how attached she felt to him.

But what kind of future could they have? He was an elephant, she was a donkey. Two different species, with wholly different ideas. And besides, he was bound to meet plenty of girls at Georgetown who were just as smart and capable as Haley, if not more so, and girls who shared his conservative worldview. His head would be turned before he even settled into his dorm.

Haley watched him holding court at the table and her heart sank further. He was so cute and, now that he knew he'd been accepted at the college of his choice, more confident than ever. And more of a catch.

Calm down, she told herself. *He's not leaving for months, and a lot can happen in that time.*

But what did she want to happen? What could possibly happen that would keep them together once he left?

She tried to smile through dinner, but she was feeling worse and worse. Alex insisted she have crème brûlée for dessert, so she ordered one, but her stomach felt so knotted up with worry she barely touched it.

As they were just finishing up, the theme from *Battlestar Galactica* suddenly blared through the restaurant, startling her. Then she realized it was only Dave's ringtone.

Dave scraped up the last of his chocolate pudding and answered the call. "Hannah? Yes? What's the matter?"

Haley could hear Hannah's panicky chipmunk voice babbling through the phone from across the table.

"Oh no!" Dave said. "Okay, I'll be right there." He clicked off. "RoBro! just short-circuited. Hannah says he's flatlining. She's freaking out. I've got to get back there."

"Really? You want to interrupt Alex's celebration dinner to tend to your robot?" Haley asked before she could stop herself.

"Haley!" Annie chastised, glaring at her friend. "You're growing more Republican red by the minute." Haley felt it coming—the inevitable split with her lefty friends and maybe even her parents if she was to stick with Alex. Suddenly, she was very confused.

"Hey, now," Alex said, defending Haley. "Let's everyone settle down and think."

Haley noticed then that Dave's eyes were actually tearing up. She should have known how much RoBro! meant to him. Although she was aware that RoBro! was just a machine, to Dave, RoBro! was his flesh-and-blood brother. Haley thought of how upset she'd be if something happened to Mitchell.

"I'll come with you, Dave," she offered. "Maybe we should bring RoBro! over to my house. My little brother, Mitchell, is actually something of an electronics whiz. He might be able to help. And in any case, he's got tons of equipment in the basement that could be useful."

"Thanks, Haley," Dave said, swallowing his tears. "You're a lifesaver."

• • •

Poor RoBro! Dave has certainly taken to his metallic sibling. It's sad, really. But does Haley have the heart to watch a friend cry or a robot die? She knows for a fact that Mitchell can take apart and fix just about anything; she's seen him do it oh so many times. (Of course, he often breaks the thing himself first, just for fun, but that's a technicality.) If you think her first priority is to bring RoBro! to her house and have Mitchell help Dave and Hannah save his electronic life, turn to page 174, ROBOT ER.

Or maybe you think the RoBro! news is sad but the Alex news is sadder. Yes, college orientation is still months away, but for the first time it feels real to Haley: Alex is going away next year. And the more time she spends with him now, helping plan inaugural balls and saving ailing robots, the more it will hurt when he finally leaves. She's already in pretty deep. If she gets too close

to him before he ships off to school, she could get her heart seriously broken. And also, the more time she spends with Alex, the more apparent their political differences become. Can they even make it as a couple, or will their polar-opposite stances on global warming and market reform clash and get in the way?

Maybe Haley should start spending more time with people in her own grade—people who will still be around come senior year. If you think Haley should protect herself emotionally and start pulling away from Alex now, before it's too late, turn to page 188, LOVE AND ROCKETS.

Robots and politicos. Politicos and robots. There was a time when Haley thought they were one and the same. Now she knows better. But that leaves her with a choice: save the robot, or save herself?

PRINCIPAL CRUM'S LITANY

April's hardly the cruelest month. January's got a heart of ice.

"People." Principal Crum had only to utter one word and titters erupted in the school auditorium. He had a bad winter cold and everything he said sounded nasally and pinched, as if he were holding his nose. Even without a cold, Principal Crum often got laughs from the kids, however—usually when he wasn't looking for them.

Principal Crum paused behind the podium, staring at his students with grave disappointment. Of course, this didn't faze them—grave disappointment was pretty much Principal Crum's default setting. Seated in a folding chair beside the podium was Ms. Underhill, the school nurse, who doubled as a phys ed teacher. In spite of the freezing January temperatures outside, and in spite of her stocky frame and thick thighs, Nurse Underhill was dressed in her usual uniform of thick-waisted short shorts and a Hillsdale Hawks T-shirt. *Not so chic,* Haley thought, well aware of why many of the students at Hillsdale called the nurse "Fatty Matty."

"I have summoned you here for this special assembly for a bery important reason," Principal Crum said. "This is not about pranks or bandalism. This is a matter of life and death. We're on Cerulean Alert, people. I repeat, Cerulean Alert."

More chuckles came from the audience after Crum announced his latest weird-color alert code. *Does he know that cerulean is pale blue?* Haley wondered. Not a very alarming color choice.

Principal Crum coughed harshly, his rheumy eyes bewildered by the crowd's reaction. *They laugh at everything, even illness,* his expression seemed to say. "This school is in the grip of an epidemic," Principal Crum continued. "A communal eating disorder that is running rampant through our halls—halls that should be a testament to the honor of our Hillsdale Hawks, not a public vomitorium!"

That really got the kids going. As the room erupted in raucous laughter, Haley glanced around from her seat on the end of a middle row. Coco, Sasha, Whitney and Cecily sat directly in front of her, looking made up and shiny. Annie, Dave and Hannah were nearer the front. Dave had a sort of shell-shocked expression on his face and Annie looked as if she were going over flash cards in her head. Up in the nosebleed section, the art crowd—Irene, Shaun, Devon and Darcy—took their usual spot, as far away from Crum as they could get.

"This is not funny, people," Principal Crum said. "This is deadly serious. The cafeteria Dumpsters are overflowing with rotting food, the uneaten lunches these lunatics among us have wasted." He glanced at Ms. Underhill, who threw him a reproving look. "And by lunatics, of course, I mean poor sick girls whom we desperately want to help." He paused, collecting himself, trying not to get too worked up. "This wastefulness is a crying shame," he began softly, his voice rising with every word. "It has also caused a raging vermin problem that is getting to be unmanageable. Do you hear that? There will soon be rats roaming the hallways if you spoiled ingrates don't do something to change your wasteful eating habits! Rats running through the hallways, people!"

Ms. Underhill glared at him again, so he added, "And by spoiled ingrates, I mean emotionally scarred young women who deserve our assistance, care and respect. Obviously."

There would have been more laughter at this

gaffe if people were still paying attention, but by now, most of them—boys especially—were texting, talking or staring at the ceiling.

"Since this is a touchy subject of a medical nature, I'd like to introduce the school nurse, Ms. Underhill, and have her take it from here. Ms. Underhill?"

Ms. Matty heaved herself off her chair and thudded like a triceratops toward the podium. Between her unflattering gym outfit and the beige skunk streak running through her black hair, she was an unsettling sight, and not exactly a vision of good dietary habits.

"Students of Hillsdale High," she said sternly. "I understand your concern with your weight. I understand that the holidays can wreak havoc on a person's figure. But many of you have taken your postholiday diets too far—way too far."

Coco leaned close to Sasha and said, "Just looking at Matty the Fatty is making me want to lose another ten." Haley couldn't help overhearing her. Ms. Underhill was not the most attractive teacher, not by a long shot, and Coco sort of had a point: looking at Nurse Underhill did take your appetite away. Haley studied Coco and the girls with her. Had she heard right? Had Coco really lost ten pounds already? She'd always been skinny; Haley wouldn't have thought Coco had ten pounds to spare. She was wearing a baggy dress, so it was hard to tell just how much weight she'd lost exactly, but from what Haley could see she seemed to be a good size smaller than her usual self. The other girls all looked thinner too.

"Girls have been passing out in the hallways from hunger," Ms. Underhill was saying. "They've been coming into my office by the dozens asking for glucose tablets to ward off low blood sugar attacks. This unhealthy behavior has got to stop immediately. From now on, if a girl comes to me with dizziness or low blood sugar, or if I even suspect she might be following one of these crazy fad diets, I'm going to call her parents and recommend therapy at the very least."

Coco, Sasha, Whitney and Cecily giggled through Ms. Underhill's speech, but Haley was pretty sure they were the ones Ms. Underhill was talking about—they and the less socially prominent girls who tried to copy the Cocobots' every move.

Haley turned around to see how many other girls looked thinner to her. Sure enough, there were a lot more prominent cheekbones and bony arms than she recalled. Her eyes finally landed in the nosebleed section, where scrawnier-than-usual Darcy Podowski was ignoring Ms. Underhill and completely focused on Devon. As in, focused with her whole self, mostly the body part of herself. Devon passively sat by making faint, unconvincing attempts to push Darcy away as she played with his hair, whispered and blew into his ear, reached across him to get something in a transparent attempt to wrap herself across his lap and more. Since Devon did almost nothing to her, Haley had to assume that he liked being ma handled by the freshman flirt.

Sickening, Haley thought. She turned away, only to catch another disturbing sight: Dave Metzger weeping. His shoulders were now shaking, his nose was running and his girlfriend, Annie, had her arm around him, trying in vain to comfort him. *Poor Dave,* Haley thought. He always wore his heart on his sleeve, if not on his stressed-out, pimply face. She suspected Dave was not crying out of sympathy for the unhealthy dieters. Something more profound was at the root of his troubles.

"Before you know it we'll have living skeletons walking through the halls of the school!" Ms. Underhill warned. "And do you have any idea what poor nutrition does to test scores?"

"Oh my," Principal Crum piped up, his voice booming from the stage. "This school cannot afford to lose a single point in its test scores! Eat, people! I want you all devouring brain food!"

This place has gone crazy, Haley thought, looking around at all the half-starved faces. *Everybody's falling apart.*

• • •

There does seem to be a lot of postholiday turmoil at Hillsdale High these days. Chalk it up to winter blues,

ve disorder, insanity, whatever—a fair ing is going around.

sual to lose weight after a breakup, Coco dumped Spencer, she has been s like a crew tossing luggage off a sink- nrough that loose-fitting dress, anyone can see she's whittling away. But then, some people find stick-thin bodies attractive. Coco seems to think Spencer does. If she's not losing weight to drive Spencer crazy, why else would she be risking her health?

If you think Coco is waaaay too skinny since her breakup with Spencer and that she's behind this unhealthy new dieting trend, turn to SKINNY BRAT on page 183. If you think Coco has reached her goal weight—and her goal of looking like a model—and feels ready to take revenge on the bad boys, turn to page 188, LOVE AND ROCKETS.

On to the next tortured soul: Dave Metzger. Why is he crying? His family life is a mess; with his mother now getting hitched to Mr. Von, that may have something to do with it. If you think Haley feels terrible for Dave and considers it her duty as a compassionate person to go see if there's anything she can do to help, turn to page 174, ROBOT ER.

Finally, Haley may be doing some suffering of her own. Does the sight of Darcy and Devon cuddling make Haley crazy jealous? If so, what can she do about it? One idea: have her punk out her look and go one-on-one with Darcy for Devon's attention. Find out if he's got attention deficit disorder when Haley is in the room on page 166, SHOWDOWN AT JACK'S.

For the poor saps of Hillsdale High, struggling to make it through another frigid winter without completely losing it, spring can't come soon enough.

RAPID RECONCILIATION

Be true to your friends, be true to your family, be true to your boyfriend, but most of all, be true to yourself.

As Reese's lips drew toward hers, Haley forgot all about the lewd pictures from the Caribbean vacation. That wasn't the Reese she knew—this was. . . . She met his lips in a sweet, warm kiss and melted. How could he have cheated, Haley thought, when he was so clearly crazy about her? Besides, Reese was hardly the lascivious type. He was a one-woman guy, and would never do anything that might hurt Haley. There must be some other logical reason. She felt it all in his lips. And as far as Haley was now concerned, she had her answer. Reese was the one for her. And she could trust him fully, even without hearing his official explanation.

As Reese cupped Haley's face in his hands and said, "There's a lot I need to tell you, but I'm so glad you came and found me, and that you trusted me. I can't tell you how happy that makes me." Haley suddenly sensed someone hovering behind her. She turned around to find Coco sneering at them.

"Isn't this sweet," Coco said snidely. "Too bad Haley came over here to dump you, Reese, for being such a lying, cheating loser."

"What?" Reese's expression shifted from blissed out to baffled. "Dump me? Haley, is that true?"

Coco smiled bitterly. "Tell him, Haley."

Haley was flustered. That kiss had pretty much obliterated her brain, so she couldn't exactly think on her feet.

"I, um—well, when I saw those pictures of you, naturally I thought at first—but, um, then, when I saw you . . ."

"What was it you called him earlier, Haley?" Coco prodded. "A no-good, two-timing fake?"

Haley looked at Reese. "I can explain."

"You were going to throw all this away, without ever hearing my side of the story?" Haley heard shock in his voice, and it surprised her. "I didn't do anything, Haley. And in your gut, you know it too."

He walked off, followed shortly thereafter by

Coco and her Coquettes, leaving Haley behind all alone in the hall. She suddenly realized she'd made a huge mistake. She'd let herself become a pawn to Coco without ever giving any hard thought to her own feelings. She'd let Coco convince her of Reese's guilt even before she'd heard his side of the story. She hadn't been loyal to anyone: not to Reese, not to her girlfriends and most of all, not to herself.

• • •

Nice job. Now Haley's got no friends, no boyfriend and no self-respect. She's a blank slate, starting over again from ground zero.

Hang your head and go back to page 1.

DEAD END

STICK WITH THE SISTERHOOD

A sister can be defined in many ways, not all of them nice.

"Ah," Coco sighed with satisfaction. "There's nothing like a girl-power mission accomplished."

Haley had gone with Coco, Sasha and Cecily to Drip coffeehouse to celebrate the successful dumping of their no-good boyfriends, and Whitney had tagged along per usual. In keeping with their diets, the girls all ordered iced green tea, even Haley, since she didn't want to invite Coco's wrath by eating in front of her. Whitney insisted they order one orange and divide it with five forks. But Haley was focusing on the divine mocha scent that kept wafting over from the next table. She glanced over with longing. A girl sat there reading a book and sipping a frothy mochaccino with chocolate shavings and whipped cream on top. There was an almond bear claw half-eaten on her plate. Haley's mouth watered. Coco, her laser vision more sharpened than ever by hunger, seemed to read Haley's mind.

"Don't even," Coco barked, snapping her fingers in front of Haley's face to bring her attention back to the diet table. "You can't let yourself be tempted by those high-calorie thigh plumpers. Just picture cellulite—or better yet, picture Fatty Matty—and the urge to binge will recede. Remember, ladies, our boys may have cheated, but we won't." Haley tried to picture cellulite and Nurse Underhill's thunder thighs, but the delicious coffee smell kept overwhelming her.

In spite of Coco's outburst, she was in a chipper mood that afternoon, basking in the glow of being responsible for at least four broken hearts, all male. "Let's have a little fun," she said. "I bet I can guess how much weight each of us has lost so far, and then we can talk about how much more we still have to lose. Of course, I know how much I've lost"—she laughed with false modesty—"almost ten pounds. It's amazing. I feel so much lighter and free! But I've got at least two more pounds to go. Let's see how well I guess with you guys." She eyeballed Sasha.

"How exactly did you calculate these figure-figures?" Sasha asked.

"Oh, I have a sense for these things," Coco insisted.

"Please." Sasha rolled her eyes, but she didn't protest. Coco studied her.

"Sasha Lewis, minus four pounds," Coco said.

Sasha's jaw dropped. "That's exactly right. How did you know?"

"When it comes to matters of the scale, just call me Coco the Clairvoyant," she joked. "Next, Whitney. You're looking . . . less than plump today. I'm guessing you've lost five pounds."

"You're right—five pounds!" Whitney said. "I weighed myself this morning."

"I win again," Coco said cheerily. "Now, Cecily. You started off pretty skinny, so you might have a harder time losing weight. My guess: minus three."

"Minus three point four," Cecily said, spearing an orange segment and popping it into her mouth. "But I feel like I should have lost twenty pounds already, I'm so hungry."

"Shhh! Don't say the h word," Coco said. "If it were easy, everybody would do it. On to Miss Haley Miller." Coco looked Haley up and down with a light smirk on her face. "Well, from the looks of your waist and hips, I would have said minus five."

"Really?" Haley said, feeling a tinge of pride. Then Coco reached over and poked her arm.

"However," Coco continued sternly. "You've clearly put on some muscle in the last week. So much so that I'm going to say plus three pounds."

"Huh?" Haley gasped. She couldn't help feeling a little insulted, especially after everybody else at the table had lost weight, though actually she had no idea what her current status was. She hadn't weighed herself recently, and instead had been just focusing on eating fewer processed foods and exercising more rigorously.

Rather than let herself get worked up over Coco's disapproving gaze, Haley decided to shrug it off. Coco could easily be right—Haley might have put on a couple of pounds as her body mass had changed from soft tissue to firm muscle. After all, it wasn't as if she were following the no-breakfast, no-dinner approach the other girls were sticking to. Haley just didn't feel well when she skipped meals. But she wasn't about to tell that to Coco.

"Well, I have been exercising more, lots of jogging and push-ups."

"Ugh, how do you have the energy?" Cecily asked.

"Haley, must I remind you?" Coco chastised. "Pilates is the only sanctioned activity."

"Oh, right," Haley said, though she had no intention of giving up her routine. She was actually enjoying her early-morning runs.

"It doesn't matter, Haley," Whitney said. "The important thing is the sisterhood."

"That's right," Coco said. "The important thing is we stuck together and dumped those boys on their horny little butts. We showed them they can't take us for granted. And now we have each other to commiserate with. Except I don't need commiseration—I feel great!"

Out of the corner of her eye Haley sensed that someone was inching toward their table. It was Hannah Moss, looking shy and nervous. Tiny Hannah was no doubt a little afraid of Coco. It wasn't unusual: lots of people were.

Hannah stopped at the table and cleared her throat. Haley smiled, trying in vain to make Hannah feel more comfortable. Coco looked up dismissively. "Yes?"

"I have a message for you, that is, there's something I think you should know," Hannah began. "My friend Alex Martin is interning for Mrs. Eton, you know, the new governor?"

"We all know who she is," Coco snapped, but she sat up a bit, taking more notice of Hannah now. "What's your message? Spit it out!"

"Okay, well, Alex told me that Mrs. Eton says Spencer dumped you. She's saying that he thought you were too controlling and that you have . . . manorexia."

"Manorexia?" Coco said. "Don't you mean anorexia?"

"No, manorexia," Hannah said. "It's a man-eating disorder, though I think she might have made that part up."

Coco's jaw dropped. She clearly was aghast. "I don't believe this. That witch!"

"It's true," Hannah said. "I assure you it is." She glanced toward the counter and saw that her to-go chai latte was ready. "Just thought you'd want to know." Hannah walked away, and as she did, Haley noticed she had a bunch of multicolored wires sticking out of her backpack. *What could they be for?* Haley wondered. *A bomb?* Hannah was, after all, a bit on the antisocial side. *But no,* Haley decided, *it must be something else.*

"I don't know whether to kill that weird little pest or save my energy to kill someone who deserves it even more," Coco said, seething. "Like Spencer. Or his mother."

"Or both," said Cecily.

"She always liked me. At least she pretended to. When Spence and I were dating, she was practically planning our wedding!"

In an astounding act of bad timing, Sasha and Whitney looked at each other with bright, excited eyes and clasped each other's hands.

"What are you two grinning about?" Cecily

asked. Haley decided all the not eating must be making her grumpy.

"We have something exciting to announce too! We can't wait any longer, it's killing us," Sasha gushed.

"Exciting?" Coco said. "You call what that tiny troll just said to me exciting?"

"We have some really amazing news to share with you," Whitney said. "We're going to be sisters!" She and Sasha squealed in unison. Coco held her ears.

"What are you talking about?" Cecily asked.

"Our parents got engaged!" Sasha said. "They called us from Tulum last night to tell us. Isn't it fantastic! I had a feeling something like this would happen when they told us they wanted to stay in Mexico another week."

"Congratulations!" Haley said. "That is so cool."

Coco flashed them a mildly pleased grin to show that she was underwhelmed by this development and that it was time to move on to the next subject. "I'm very happy for you both. It's not like anything's really going to change all that much, since you already live together, but I suppose shopping for matching bridesmaid dresses will be a kick. Next topic."

Wedding news obviously didn't sit well with Coco, since she'd just broken up with her boyfriend. On top of that, she'd just learned that said boyfriend's mother, who wasn't just some PTA mom but the actual governor of New Jersey, was spreading nasty rumors about her, rumors that everyone was likely to believe were true.

"What are we going to do for Valentine's Day?" Whitney chirped in a feeble attempt to follow Coco's wishes. "Now that we're all single ladies on the prowl, I mean. . . ."

Another possible sore subject, Haley thought, but tact was never Whitney's strong suit.

Sasha looked at Haley. "That's Haley's seventeenth birthday, isn't it? We need to come up with something really special this year."

"Haley will be getting wheels!" Whitney squealed.

"Thank goodness," Coco said. "I'm sick of always having to pick you up and drive you all over town."

"Nothing's for sure yet," Haley said, trying to manage expectations. Her parents had mentioned something about a surprise in the driveway for her birthday. She hoped they knew better than to give her a bike, but with her parents she could never be sure. "But I have a good feeling."

• • •

So, Sasha and Whitney are finally going to make it legal—they're about to become stepsisters. That is major news—to Sasha and Whitney. Clearly Coco finds it less than earth-shattering. If you think Coco's reaction

to Sasha and Whitney's supermonumental news was really bratty, turn to page 183, SKINNY BRAT.

If you think Coco has a legitimate excuse—she's preoccupied with Hannah's update on Mrs. Eton calling her a man-eating beast—witness as Coco proves that two can play at that game on page 188, LOVE AND ROCKETS. Finally, if you're curious as to what Hannah Moss was doing with all those crazy wires sticking out of her backpack, find out on page 174, ROBOT ER.

SLIMMING EFFECT

Beware the easy perfection promised by a pill.

"I got these pills from my trainer at the gym," Coco said, patting the designer vial she pulled from her purse. "They give you energy and bind with toxins to flush them out of your system. I've never felt purer! Or more alive!"

So that's her secret, Haley thought, eyeing Coco's pill bottle enviously. Coco was only dropping so much weight and still feeling great because of a chemical supplement. Haley had watched in admiration for seven days straight as Coco had survived without injesting a single bite of solid food—other than the occasional orange segment. Coco claimed to be on a liquids-only diet, and yet didn't seem to be any the worse for it. Especially in the past few days. She looked healthy and appeared to have plenty of vim and vigor.

"You should try it, Haley," Coco said. "It will totally clean you out."

Haley did think Coco's skin had miraculously gotten clearer and her eyes brighter midway through the cleanse. *Maybe I will try it,* she decided as Coco poured a pile of pills into Haley's hand.

For the next three days, Haley felt great. She had tons of energy, so much so that her homework was usually done by six p.m., and she still had time to clean her room and help her mom with the dishes. She weighed herself daily and the pounds were finally falling off. Haley could suddenly fit into clothes she hadn't worn since middle school.

Avoiding food in front of her parents wasn't easy, but Haley fooled them by pushing her fork around and talking animatedly throughout the dinner hour. If Joan and Perry were busy laughing, she reasoned, they wouldn't notice her insignificant caloric intake. Haley was amazed at her own self-control. She felt as though she could do anything! If she could stop eating, what couldn't she do? Her body was at her disposal, completely. It didn't tell her what to do—she told her body what to do. And it obeyed.

At the end of day three of popping pills, Haley had dropped a miraculous seven pounds, and yet she still felt strong and vibrant enough to take a run after school. She zipped around her neighborhood, and then, still feeling great, added another couple of miles onto her route. By the time she got home, her heart was thumping like a rabbit's. She walked through her front door to find her mother and father sitting in the living room with Principal Crum.

"What's going on?" she asked. It wasn't her birthday quite yet, so it couldn't be a surprise party. . . .

"This is an intervention," Principal Crum said. "Your family and friends have been worried about you, Haley."

"You've been starving yourself, honey," Joan Miller said. "We want to help you before it goes too far. Your father found these in your bedroom." Joan pulled out the stash of pills.

"The point is," Perry Miller said, "that when your body tells you it's hungry, you need to listen, Snoodles. We don't want you to get sick."

Hearing her father call her by her childhood nickname brought tears to Haley's eyes, and she realized how dangerous her quest to be stick thin had been. Her parents were right—she hadn't been in control after all. She'd only been blindly following Coco's lead.

"I'm sorry to break this to you, Haley, but we've

booked you for a two-week stay at a nearby psychiatric facility," Principal Crum announced.

"What?" Haley asked, shocked.

"We can't have you influencing the other girls at school," Principal Crum continued.

"But a psych ward? Really?"

"Haley, look at yourself. You're skin and bones," Joan pleaded.

"We'll visit you every day, Snoodles," Perry added. "And you won't be alone up there. Coco De Clerq checked herself in this morning."

● ● ●

What were you thinking, pushing the already-thin Haley to starve herself and resort to dangerous appetite suppressants? She could have ended up someplace far worse than a psych ward, like the emergency room or even the morgue. Hang your head and go back to page 1.

DEAD END

SHOWDOWN AT JACK'S

"Indecisive" is code for "easily manipulated."

"Remember—when you see Devon, play it cool," Irene commanded.

"I've got it, Irene," Haley said. "You've only reminded me, like, a hundred times."

"But it's crucial," Irene said. "I don't want you to take one look at him and melt like you usually do, or the whole plan's a bust."

They were lingering outside Jack's Vintage Clothing, where Devon worked, for a little last-minute strategizing. Also, Haley thought, they were putting off going inside. She was nervous. If Irene's plan didn't work, Haley would look like an idiot. Who knew—maybe she already looked like one. Irene had transformed her into a punk-glam goddess, with a green streak in her hair, heavy eye makeup, a schoolgirl mini-kilt and combat boots. Her brother, Mitchell, had almost screamed when he saw her. Haley hoped Devon would have a friendlier reaction.

"Ready?" Irene asked. Irene normally dressed punk, but for Operation Showdown she'd really gone all out. She had on a hot black T-shirt dress ripped strategically at the shoulder and purple sparkles dusted below her eyebrows.

Haley nodded and took a deep breath. "Ready. Let's go."

They threw open the door of the store and walked in as if they owned the place. Devon was at his post behind the counter, and Darcy was sitting on top of it next to the register, lounging catlike in front of him. Haley tried not to look, but she couldn't help but notice that when she and Irene walked in, Darcy grabbed Devon by the neck, pulled his face toward hers and started whispering in his ear.

Irene led Haley to the glam racks and started rummaging. She yanked a tiny purple dress off a hanger and held it up against Haley's body. "You could totally rock this," Irene said. "Go try it on. I'll keep looking. You need something superhot for the show tonight."

Haley ambled past the counter on her way to the dressing room. Devon stared at her, and then his mouth fell open.

"Haley?" he said. "I almost didn't recognize you."

Haley barely glanced at him. "Oh, hey."

Darcy was still clinging to his neck. Devon wrested himself away so suddenly she nearly tumbled off the counter.

Haley put on the purple dress. It barely grazed her thighs, but it did look hot with her recently enhanced curves and with the black tights she was wearing. She stepped out of the dressing room to model it for Irene. She didn't even glance Devon's way but she knew full well he was watching.

"What do you think?" Haley turned like a spokesmodel in front of Irene. "Is it right for the concert?"

"I love it," Irene said. "But I love these more." She dumped a pair of silver pleather pants and a silver halter top into Haley's arms. "Get back in there."

Haley marched back into the dressing room and put on the skintight outfit. She and Irene were purposely mentioning this mysterious "concert" in hopes that it would pique Devon's interest. As the coup de grace of Irene's devilish plan, Shaun had scored front-row seats to the Meat Puppets' revival show in Manhattan that night. The Meat Puppets just happened to be Devon's obsession of the moment.

Haley emerged from the dressing room to model the silver outfit. "I look like one of the X-Men," she whispered to Irene. "You can see every bump on my body."

"Those 'bumps' are called curves, and you look unbelievably hot," Irene countered. "Maybe too hot, if that's possible."

Haley was dying to steal a glimpse at Devon to see if he was catching all this. Irene winked to let her know he definitely was. Haley could hear Darcy's distress from across the store.

"Devon. Devon!" Darcy snapped. "Over here! I asked you a question."

"Sorry, Darcy," Devon said. "Um, the answer is . . . I don't know."

"You don't know what time you get off today?"

"Yeah, that's right. . . ."

Irene shot Haley a conspiratorial grin. Their plan was working perfectly. The sight of Haley in these sexy punk outfits had Devon so addled he barely remembered his name.

Haley tried on some towering platform shoes with a low-cut T-shirt and tight black pants, and a curve-hugging dress with strategically placed cutouts, all the while studiously ignoring Devon. When it was time to check out she said loudly, "Everything fits so well, I don't know which one to buy."

"That's the beauty of vintage," Irene said. "Super-cheap. Let's get them all!"

They lugged their haul over to the counter. Haley was face to face with Devon at last. Darcy was still stretched out on the counter, pouting.

"Can you get down off the counter, Darcy?" Devon said. "We need the space."

She hopped off, glaring at Haley. "I wouldn't get those silver pants if I were you," she said. "You don't have the legs for them."

"Are you kidding?" Devon said. "That outfit looked like it was made for her."

"What's our total?" Irene said impatiently.

Devon rang up the purchases. "So what show are you going to see tonight?"

"Uh, Meat Puppets," Irene said. "Shaun scored us front row seats."

"What? Why didn't he tell me? He knows I'm way into them." Devon looked hurt.

"I guess he figured you'd be busy," Irene said, casting a meaningful glance at Darcy.

"I'd drop anything to see them," Devon said.

Irene shrugged. "Sorry. Shaun wanted to invite you but he couldn't get a fifth ticket, and we didn't want anyone to feel left out." Another sly glance at Darcy, who bristled.

"What are you talking about?" Devon said. "I feel left out." He followed Irene's eyes to Darcy and connected the dots. "Oh."

"Anyway, thanks." Irene picked up one shopping bag and Haley took the other. "See you."

Irene and Haley gave him a breezy goodbye and headed for the door. Behind them Haley heard Darcy mew, "Don't worry, Dev—at least you've got me. I'll be hanging here with you. All. Night. Long. Isn't that better than some stupid concert?"

Irene pushed open the door and called out behind her, "Don't work too hard, Devon!" Both girls giggled as they looked back once more. Devon was slumped behind the counter, looking miserable. Darcy was trying to recapture his attention, but at that point, Devon no longer seemed so taken with her.

"That ought to do it," Irene said as she and Haley ran laughing down the street. "Darcy came off as a total liability—a leech! He'll never look at her the same way again."

"I don't know," Haley said. "We may have put a wedge between him and Darcy, but that doesn't mean he's mine yet."

• • •

Looks as though Irene's little plan worked. Devon is definitely sour on Darcy and suddenly sees Haley in a

new light. But the question still lingers: is this what Haley really wants? Sure, Devon seems to be interested in Haley now, but what about later? How far is he willing to go? Will he fight to win Haley over and give up Darcy for good? Or is he the kind of passive guy who only loves the one he's with, whoever that might be? Haley is putting a lot of effort into turning his head. But now she has to decide if all this effort is worth the reward.

Another variable is Darcy. She's clearly spinning a twisted web over Devon, and is not likely to give him up so easily. Does Haley want to get caught up in Darcy's schemes—or would she be better off getting out now before she's in too deep?

If Haley loses her enthusiasm for punk-glam, there are other boys she could focus her energies on. Super-smart senior Alex Martin may not be the cool artsy type, but he obviously cares about Haley and isn't afraid to show it. Then there's always Reese Highland. He has a big basketball game coming up. Haley could show up and surprise him—it might reignite their relationship after a prolonged holiday chill. On the other hand, Reese has said many times that he doesn't like surprises on big-game days.

If you want to see whether Devon's willing to work to win Haley over, turn to page 193, HOT PURSUIT. If you think he isn't worth all this trouble, trade him in for a CANDLELIT BIRTHDAY date with Alex Martin on page 203. Finally, if you think Reese is the ultimate one for Haley, send her off to watch him play basketball on page 210, RIDGEWOOD RIVALS. So what if he's not big on surprises—that doesn't apply to Haley, does it?

Even mechanical siblings can be a pain in the butt.

Dave and Hannah wheeled RoBro! into the Millers' basement, where Haley had set up a triage cot for him. Mitchell, who had few social skills but was a mechanical whiz beyond his seven years, was setting up his equipment. It was past his bedtime, but Haley had managed to convince their parents that this was a real medical emergency.

Dave pressed his fingers against RoBro!'s neck. "There's no pulse!" he cried, tears welling in his eyes. "He's gone! I killed him. I've killed RoBro!"

Annie rushed to his side to comfort him. He may have been a robot, but to Dave, RoBro! was as real as any other brother.

"Don't give up yet," Mitchell said. "I can take care of this. Haley, screwdriver, stat."

Haley stared in confusion at the ten screwdrivers of all shapes and sizes arrayed in Mitchell's toolbox. "Which one?"

"Size-three Phillips head, dummy!" Mitchell snapped. "Hurry up! We're racing against the clock here!"

Haley grabbed something that looked as though it could be a size-three Phillips head and handed it to her little brother, guessing that his next oddball obsession phase was probably going to be emergency surgeons.

"Hand out those surgical masks and scrubs," he barked at Haley. "I want everybody wearing them—no exceptions. If RoBro!'s circuits are corrupted by airborne organic matter it could be disastrous."

"How so?" Hannah asked.

"Well, RoBro! could turn . . . evil. Or he could develop a taste for human flesh," Mitchell warned as Hannah rolled her eyes.

Haley handed around the surgical masks and scrubs and everyone put them on.

"What do you mean, evil?" Alex asked.

"He could become his own evil twin," Mitchell

said with a completely serious face. "We'll know if it happens if his eyes glow red."

"I thought I saw a red gleam in them before he conked out," Dave said in a panicky voice. "Oh no! What have I done?"

Haley didn't know who was crazier, Mitchell for his wild imagination or Dave for taking it all seriously. But the mood in the room was so tense, and RoBro! clearly meant so much to Dave, she felt she had to play along. Besides, she had total faith in Mitchell's ability to fix the bot.

He unscrewed RoBro!'s chest panel and opened it up. "Haley, my drill, please. Stand back, everybody. This could throw some sparks."

The group gave Mitchell his space while he drilled and hammered and tinkered with the robot. "Your brother is quite a character," Alex whispered to Haley.

"Yup," she replied. "Straight out of a bad science fiction movie."

Forty-five minutes later, Mitchell pulled down his mask and stepped away from the robot. "I think I've done it. We'll find out in a minute. Dave, why don't you try turning him on?"

Dave stepped forward and pressed RoBro!'s on button. Everyone watched breathlessly. Nothing happened for a second. Then RoBro! hummed to life. His metallic body shifted, almost as if he were breathing. Suddenly, he sat up, lifted his arms and laid them over Dave's shoulders in a robot hug.

"I am. Feeling much. Bet-ter now," RoBro! said in his robot voice. Everyone gasped in amazement.

"He's well!" Dave cried. "He's alive!"

"Thank you. Brother David," RoBro! finished.

Dave wiped tears from his eyes and hugged the robot. Annie, Hannah, Alex and Haley applauded. Mitchell nodded his head modestly.

"What can I say? I hate to lose a patient," he said.

"That was very stirring," Alex said.

"Really touching," Annie added.

"We should celebrate RoBro!'s return to life," Haley said. "Anybody want some ice cream?"

"I do!" Annie said.

"Well, sorry, we don't have any ice cream," Haley said. "But we do have zucchini bread."

They all trooped upstairs to the kitchen. Haley sliced and toasted the mildly sweet veggie bread for all of her guests. Dave requested a small piece for RoBro!—"Just a teensy one, since he's still recovering. He can't eat it, of course, but he does like to smell things."

"There's been so much drama, I almost forgot about your big news, Alex," Haley said as she finally settled down at the table. Earlier that evening they'd all been celebrating Alex's acceptance to Georgetown, though that felt like ages ago now.

"It's a good night for everyone, isn't it?" Alex said.

"It certainly is!" Annie said. "So how are things going for Team Eton? And can you get me one of those Devon McKnight T-shirts? They're the hottest thing at school right now."

Eleanor Eton had recently charged Alex with renewing Spencer's social standing, which had plummeted after Coco De Clerq publicly dumped him. So Alex had hired the talented artist Devon McKnight to design a pro-Spencer shirt to counteract Coco's smear campaign. Devon had created an edgy instant classic, and soon everybody at school was wearing them—if they weren't sporting a preppier Team Coco shirt.

At the mere mention of Devon's name, Haley felt a pang in her stomach. Those Team Eton T-shirts had brought her scruffy classmate into the limelight and made the artsy/creative junior suddenly cool. Haley had been spending so much time with these science and political brainiacs lately that she sometimes felt she was neglecting her artistic side, and to her, Devon represented this freer, alternate version of her life. Plus, he was way cute. She thought she'd stomped out the flame of that old crush a while ago, but maybe not. Clearly, there was still a kernel of feeling intact.

"That reminds me, I've got to ask Devon to make some more," Alex said. "I'm giving them away for free but at this point I could sell them, they're so popular."

"Is Mrs. Eton really paying you to make Spencer a teen idol again?" Hannah asked. "Don't you think that's kind of unethical?"

"It's hard to say," Alex said evasively. "But it's good experience for me. It's like a microcosm of a political campaign. I try to look at Spencer as a candidate. I don't have to like him personally. I just have to convince the voters—or the kids at school—to like him."

Just then, Joan Miller came in and sliced herself a nibble of zucchini bread. "Sorry to break up the party, but I've got to march your mechanic off to bed now. It's getting very late."

"Thanks for saving RoBro!, Mitchell," Dave said. "You're a genius, and I don't use that term lightly."

"No problem," Mitchell said. "I was only doing my duty. I took an oath; I must do everything in my power to save a sick machine. Good night, everyone."

Haley and Alex helped Dave and Hannah load the revived RoBro! into Annie's car. After they drove away, Alex lingered in the driveway.

"I'm very impressed by your brother's electronic skills," Alex said. "That was amazing, what he did tonight."

"I just feel lucky to have a real brother, and not one I had to build out of scrap metal."

"Me too," Alex said. "I can't imagine being an only child. No wonder Dave and Annie are so . . . odd." He leaned against his car, not quite ready to leave yet. "So listen—what are you doing on Valentine's Day?"

Valentine's Day, eh? Interesting question, Haley thought. She felt her cheeks heat up. "Actually, that's my birthday. I'm turning seventeen."

"Easy birthday to remember," Alex said. "I was wondering if you'd like to join me for dinner at my house. A special dinner in honor of your birthday and the day of hearts. I'll cook. I'll take a stab at it, anyway. You will be witness to my very first steak au poivre."

"Wow," Haley said. "What a lovely invitation." In the background she heard the sound of a basketball bouncing on asphalt. She glanced across the yard to her next-door neighbors' driveway. The light was on over the Highlands' garage, and there was Reese practicing free throws in a ski hat, hoodie and his varsity basketball shorts. He bounced the ball twice, shot and *whoosh,* made it in.

Haley knew the basketball team had a major game coming up. It was kind of sweet to see Reese working so hard for it, practicing by himself late at night in the freezing cold.

"My parents will be out of town with both my brothers," Alex said. "So if you don't come, I'll be all alone on Valentine's Day."

Haley smiled. "Now, that would be a shame."

"A terrible shame," Alex said. "So what do you say?"

• • •

Hmm . . . Haley could have her birthday plans all sewn up—if she wants to. A boy has just offered to cook dinner for her—what could be better? Still, a combo seventeenth birthday/Valentine's Day is a big event. Haley is sure to get other offers for that evening, at least from her friends. What should she do?

The big basketball game against Ridgewood is coming up. It must be important if Reese is so worried about it he's shooting free throws in the middle of the night. Maybe he could use Haley's support. They haven't really been talking lately, but that could change if Haley shows up at the game. Then again, maybe he doesn't want any distractions.

Then there's Devon and his cool new T-shirt business. Haley has always had a little thing for him, and for a time, he seemed to like her too, but lately he's been so passive about it. Maybe his association with Alex is a sign that he's finally gotten his act together. Maybe, if Haley makes a little effort now, things could be different between them.

If you're sure Haley would love to have Alex cook dinner for her on her birthday, especially if his parents aren't home, turn to page 203, CANDLELIT BIRTHDAY.

If you think Haley should support Reese at his game,

turn to page 210, RIDGEWOOD RIVALS. Finally, if you think Haley thinks Devon's new T-shirt business is the coolest thing at school, go find out how he's feeling about Haley these days on page 193, HOT PURSUIT.

Boys, boys, boys! It's a tough job to choose, but somebody has to do it.

SKINNY BRAT

Keep your friends close and your enemies closer— and don't let your frenemies out of your sight.

"Doesn't Coco look great?" Whitney said. "She's so skinny!"

"I don't know . . . ," Haley said. They watched Coco sashay down the hall, surprisingly full of pep for a girl who'd hardly eaten in more than a week. As far as Haley was concerned, Coco had gone from skinny to too skinny to waaaay too skinny since she'd broken up with Spencer. It was typical of Whitney to think "the skinnier the better" when it came to Coco's looks. Whitney had once been a rabid binge-and-purger, and even though she'd recovered, Haley wasn't sure her body-image issues were fully resolved yet.

"Are you going to the big basketball game?" Whitney asked, bouncing from subject to subject in her usual spacy manner. "I really want to go, but since half the boys on the team are our enemies now, I'm not sure what to do."

"Me either," Haley said. The Hillsdale varsity boys' team had a major game coming up against their rival, Ridgewood High, on February 14, and Haley hated to miss it—even though that night was not only Valentine's Day but also her birthday, and there were sure to be other fun things to do. To complicate matters, she and Reese were on the outs lately. She just wasn't sure the game was worth the angst.

"Now that you guys dumped your boyfriends, it feels like there are no boys left in school to talk to," Whitney complained. "I wish we could meet some new boys and start over."

"I know what you mean," Haley said.

Coco stopped to chat with a few senior girls, who were clearly complimenting her on her appearance. Haley had to admit that lately, Coco was looking more and more like the twig-thin models her ex-boyfriend Spencer had gotten caught with over winter break.

"I wonder how many calories she eats a day," Whitney said, spooning raspberry yogurt into her mouth.

"So do I," Haley said. "In fact, I think I'll try to find out." Haley had a bad feeling Coco was dropping pounds in a very unhealthy way. She decided to trail her and find out just how Coco was shedding so much weight so quickly, with so much peppy energy to spare. *No time like the present,* Haley thought, following Coco into the cafeteria to see what her friend would choose to eat. Coco sat down with Sasha, then pulled a bottle of cloudy liquid from her bag. When Sasha wasn't looking, Coco proceeded to pop several multicolored capsules into her mouth.

"Ahem, what is that stuff?" Haley asked, sitting down with them.

"What, this? It's just part of my cleansing program," Coco said defensively. "Hot water, lemon juice, cayenne pepper and a little maple syrup for energy. You should try it—it's great."

"No thanks," Haley said. "And that's not what I meant."

Coco shot Haley a threatening glance that said, *Mind your own business.*

"What are you talking about, Haley?" Sasha asked, mildly annoyed. "Don't be vague, please? All this dieting has wreaked havoc on my ability to concentrate."

"I saw Coco taking pills," Haley revealed.

"What are you, the lunch police?" Coco snapped. "Don't worry, this is all perfectly healthy. My trainer at the gym gave them to me."

"They're from Trainer Bobby? Then they must be okay," Sasha said sarcastically. "That guy sells steroids to half the football team."

"Haley, the whole point of a cleanse is the special chemical reaction certain ingredients have on your system," Coco insisted. "I know what I'm doing."

Coco could say "Don't worry" all she wanted, but Haley and Sasha were officially worried. This cleanse was obviously a front for a starvation diet with chemical enhancement. Haley was afraid that Coco might have entered an early stage of anorexia. Not eating at all seemed even more pernicious than Whitney's flirtation with bulimia.

Should I do something about this? Haley wondered. *But if so, what? And what if getting involved means causing more harm than good?*

• • •

Coco's calorie crunching has clearly gone too far, but what should Haley do about it? If you think she should talk to Coco directly, in private, CONFRONT COCO on page 217. On the other hand, confronting her could backfire. Coco has a very controlling personality and does not always welcome Haley's input. If you think Haley should stay out of this one, especially knowing how cranky Coco's been acting lately, CALL THE NURSE on page 223.

If you think Haley should forget about Coco's

problems and go spy on Reese's basketball performance instead, turn to page 210, RIDGEWOOD RIVALS. Finally, if you want to meet some new boys from another school and forget all about the hotties of Hillsdale High for a while, turn to page 227, MUSICAL VALENTINE.

LOVE AND ROCKETS

Love is not a team sport, but revenge can be.

Haley was shocked when she walked down the hall at school and spotted Coco pressed against Devon in a corner. What was that about? Haley bristled. No way was Coco into Devon, and no way Devon was into Coco. But why was she whispering seductively into his ear?

On closer inspection, Coco wasn't whispering at all, she was commanding. Devon was wearing a Team Coco T-shirt he'd made as a joking commentary on Coco's war against Spencer. Coco loved the shirt and, from what Haley overheard, she was asking—no, demanding—no, begging—Devon to produce as many more of them as he could. Coco would even foot the bill; Devon could hand out the shirts to the student body for free.

"How many more?" Devon asked.

"Let's start with three hundred," Coco said.

"No problemo," Devon said. "For the right price."

It turned out Devon was making the shirts at Jack's, the vintage clothing store where he worked after school, using an old silk-screening machine Jack had recently bought and handed over to Devon to use.

"Money is no object," Coco said. "I want this school flooded with Team Coco tees by the end of the week." She stuffed a wad of bills into Devon's pocket and walked away.

Devon caught Haley watching and grinned. "Jackpot," he said, winking at her flirtatiously.

"Looks like someone's found a new source of income," Haley said, marveling at how confident and alluring Devon suddenly seemed.

"How can I say no to cold, hard cash," he said, throwing up his hands. "Maybe you'll let me buy you dinner one of these days."

Haley blushed as he walked away without waiting for her answer.

Devon was as good as his word. By the end of the week, Haley noticed Team Coco shirts all over school.

Coco used them as a conversation starter—and the conversation usually went something like this:

"Did you know I dumped Spencer's sorry butt right after New Year's? I don't care if his mother is governor, he's a total deadbeat. He'll be lucky if he even graduates next year. All he does is smoke pot and drink his way through school. Oh, and did I tell you, he's got problems in the bedroom? Yeah, no wonder he orchestrated all those shots of him with those models in Nevis. It's like he has to prove his manhood or something."

The exchange usually ended up with the classmate joining in with Coco's insults and then complimenting her polished taste and sense of style, which made Coco beam with joy. Meanwhile, Spencer skulked around the school like a wanted criminal, avoiding social confrontations whenever possible. Not like the superconfident, even egotistical, old Spencer at all.

Apparently, Alex Martin had noticed the shirts too. "Mrs. Eton was wondering why Spencer hasn't seemed like himself lately," Annie Armstrong reported to Haley. "So Alex told her about the Coco shirts and the rumors she's been spreading about Spencer. So Mrs. Eton told Alex to fix the situation immediately and handed him a stack of petty cash."

"But how's he supposed to fix it?" Haley asked. Alex had a thing for Haley, it was true, and she had personally witnessed him performing miracu[illegible] feats in his attempts to get her to date him. Bu[illegible] restoring Spencer's street cred after Coco publicly shamed him? Even Haley thought the job might exceed Alex's abilities.

"He's going to bribe Devon to halt production temporarily on Team Coco shirts and switch over to make Team Eton shirts—with an even cooler design, of course," Annie said.

"Wow, Devon must be swimming in money," Haley mused out loud.

"That must be a new feeling for him," Annie said.

By the next day, the first hundred Team Eton T-shirts appeared. Soon there was an all-out battle taking place in the halls of Hillsdale High. As Team Eton shirts sprouted everywhere, especially on boys supporting Spencer's lavish bachelor lifestyle, Coco fought back with ever more Team Coco shirts, in baby-doll sizes and appealing bright colors. The school became divided into Coco and Eton camps and, Haley soon realized, you could be on only one team or the other. You had to state your position.

Coco even reinstated her blacklist. She roamed the halls with a clipboard in hand, monitoring student loyalties. She wrote down the name of every boy or girl she caught wearing a pro-Spencer shirt, and she didn't count "irony" as an acceptable excuse. You were either with her or against her, and either way, she would never, ever forget it.

• • •

aley do? Do you think she should invest ler sympathies may lie with Coco, but think of Coco's methods? Is Coco taking this revenge thing too far, or not far enough? And if Haley doesn't join in the boy bashing, will she lose a spot in the sisterhood?

Haley's big seventeenth birthday is coming up, and she's got a few decisions to make about how to spend it.

If you think Coco has done a great job of alienating the boys, who totally deserve it, and that Haley should join the sisterhood to take revenge even farther, turn to page 227, MUSICAL VALENTINE. Haley's got other boys besides Spencer to think about. If you think she was impressed with how Alex jumped right into Spencer's social life and saved his reputation, turn to page 203, CANDLELIT BIRTHDAY, to help Haley turn seventeen in a romantic setting with a smart high school senior. Lastly, if you think Devon's business model and creativity were by far the coolest aspects of this whole battle of the sexes, turn to HOT PURSUIT on page 193 to see if Devon makes an effort on Haley's birthday this year.

HOT PURSUIT

Cold fish are just as tasty as any other, once they've sizzled over the coals.

"What do you mean, you want more?" Irene said. "Devon obviously likes you. He's spending less and less time with Darcy. You've practically got him in the palm of your hand."

"I guess," Haley said. "But I want him to obsess over me. I want to know he's chosen me of his own free will, and that he doesn't have even an ounce of regret." They were hanging out by their lockers after art class, watching a parade of Team Coco and Team

Eton shirts go by. Haley was sick and tired of waiting for Devon to get up the nerve—or energy, or whatever it was he lacked—to show her how he really felt about her. She kept thinking he liked her a whole whole lot, but he was always too chicken to do anything about it.

"Just keep doing what you've been doing," Irene said. "And he'll obsess over you, believe me. Keep playing it cool. Always. Never show any kind of reaction if possible, good or bad. If you absolutely must respond, err on the side of being a malcontent."

"But won't that turn him off after a while?" Haley asked. "Won't he just think I'm a brat?"

"Just the opposite," Irene said. "With someone as shy and detached as Devon, you have to beat him at his own game. You have to master his art form."

"His art form?"

"That whole 'too tragically hip to communicate' shtick he uses to keep everyone at arm's length. Like, 'I'm too deep to talk to girls as if I like them. I'm too deep to date.' You know what I'm talking about."

Haley knew exactly what Irene was talking about. Devon's too-cool attitude had been driving her crazy all year.

"Just remember," Irene said, "even when Devon starts to show signs of liking you, act like you don't care in the least. Like you barely even notice him. He's totally under your radar. Got it?"

"Got it."

That afternoon, as Devon was walking to his car to head to Jack's, he spotted Haley across the parking lot and called out, "Later, Haley." She didn't respond. In fact, she acted as if she hadn't even heard him speak.

Devon stopped in his tracks. "Haley?" he yelled. "Need a ride?"

The hair on the back of her neck tingled. Irene's plan was working already! Devon rarely offered her a ride home. She wanted to say, "Yes! And guess what? My birthday's coming up and I'm going to get my license and maybe a car of my own! And then I can offer you a ride. I'm so excited!" But a cucumber would never gush that way, and she was supposed to stay cucumber-cool. A reaction like that would have been highly uncool.

Instead, Haley kept her composure and didn't look up from the book she was reading. She just shook her head and said, "No thanks."

She played the cool game for three days in a row. By the following week, the week of her birthday, which was also Valentine's Day, Devon was showing clear signs of interest. "Don't get excited," Irene warned her. "Don't react. Just keep telling yourself: I don't like him. I don't care about him. He's a slug under the heel of my boot."

"A slug under the heel of my boot," Haley echoed. "But look!" She pulled a homemade CD out of her backpack. She'd found it in her locker that morning with a note from Devon: *I just threw this together. Some of my favorites. Thought it might make a nice sound track for your b-day.*

"A mix CD!" Haley nearly squealed. "And it has the most amazing songs on it. The last one is, like, totally romantic."

"Haley, listen," Irene said, shaking her. "Snap out of it. Stick to the plan. Remember: do not react. Don't even thank him for it. It's just a stupid CD. It probably cost seventy-five cents and took him, like, three minutes to burn."

"Don't thank him for it?" Haley said. "But isn't that rude?"

"It's totally rude," Irene said. "And it's going to make him crazy for you. You're building up tension, like putting air inside a balloon. If you get all gushy on him now, he'll lose interest so fast it'll be like letting the balloon go before you've tied it off with a knot. All the air will rush out and what have you got? A limp, soggy piece of rubber."

"Ew, I don't want that," Haley said.

"No, trust me, you don't."

When Devon saw Haley in the art room later that day and said, "Hey, did you get the CD I left you?" Haley barely glanced at him.

"The what?" she said.

"The CD. With songs on it? I made it for you myself."

"Oh, that. Is that what it was?" Haley said in her coldest voice. "Um, thanks." It took every ounce of strength not to tell him how she really felt. She did, however, allow herself to sneak a peek at Devon's baffled face before he turned away. He looked miserable. The pressure was starting to build.

On Valentine's Day, Devon walked up to Haley at her locker and cleared his throat nervously. She thought he was wearing a slightly more carefully chosen outfit than usual. Still slouchy, but the vintage blazer was pretty sharp and more formal than his usual ratty sweatshirt.

"Hey—I hear it's your birthday," Devon said.

Inside Haley's head a voice squealed, *Oh my God, he remembered my birthday!* She couldn't wait to find out what kind of surprise he had in store for her. But Irene's stern voice overrode Haley's excitement. *Remember: do not react at all,* she reminded herself.

"Yeah, it's today," Haley said in as blasé a manner as she could muster.

"Well, listen," Devon said. "There's this photo show at MoMA I've been really interested in seeing, and I was wondering . . . I was wondering if you wanted to come with me. We could make a night of it, you know. . . . The museum's open till eight, and then we could grab something to eat in the city. . . ."

Haley was dying to say yes, but she controlled herself, Irene-style. "Sorry, I can't," she said coldly. "I've got a family obligation."

"Oh. Okay." Her heart both ached and was thrilled to see the disappointment on Devon's face. "Maybe another time, then."

She didn't answer, so he walked away dejectedly. She sighed as she watched him go. Irene's plan wasn't easy. She would have loved to spend her birthday in the city with Devon. But according to Irene, he wasn't smitten enough yet. She had to soldier on.

After school that day, Haley's dad picked her up and drove her to the DMV. She took her driver's test and passed. She was a little shaky on three-point turns, but the woman scoring her road test didn't seem to pick up on it. At the end of the test, Haley ran outside to the waiting room and waved her brand-new driver's license at her dad.

"Congratulations!" He gave her a big hug. "My little girl's a driver. Want to chauffeur me home?"

Haley carefully maneuvered her parents' hybrid from the DMV for the twenty blocks or so to her own street. She was beginning to feel comfortable behind the wheel when, right as she turned into her driveway, she nearly rear-ended a hideous car that was blocking the garage. It was a large, pale yellow sedan covered with bumper stickers like "I Brake for

Cookies," "Lady in a Walker on Board" and "Sunday Drivers = Safe Drivers." Haley recognized it instantly as her grandmother's old Lemon, famous for the way it backfired every few feet.

"Is Gam Polly here for my birthday?" Haley asked enthusiastically. "If that's the case, I'll forgive her for parking her giant monstrosity of a car in my parking space."

"That giant monstrosity . . . is your new car!" Perry announced. "Happy seventeenth birthday, Snoodles!"

"What?" Haley was stunned. She'd been hoping for a car—a new car. Barring that, she'd been hoping for something she wouldn't be too embarrassed to be seen in. But this—this was a travesty. Her worst nightmare, on wheels. "You say that like it's a good thing."

Her father laughed. "It's all yours, Haley. You deserve it."

You mean I deserve to be punished? she thought. *Because that's what this feels like.*

"Yay," she said halfheartedly, purely for her father's benefit.

Her birthday dinner with the family that night cheered her up a little. Haley knew she shouldn't sulk about getting Gam Polly's clunker instead of a cool new ride, like the one Coco got on her birthday or even Annie Armstrong's tiny electric car. She supposed the Lemon was better than no car, and she tried to be a good sport about it.

Right after dinner, the doorbell rang. Her parents were busy in the kitchen so Haley ran to get it. When she opened the door, there stood Devon holding a big red gift box tied with a red ribbon.

"Hi," he said, grinning at her.

"Hey," she said coolly. Keeping up her icy veneer was harder than ever. She was so disappointed over the car that the prospect of a surprise from Devon was all the more appealing.

He paused, glancing down at the red box, then said, "I got you something. For your birthday."

"Huh," she muttered with all the lack of interest she could muster. She stepped outside and closed the door, making a point of refusing to let him in. He pressed the box into her hands. She sat on the cold front steps to open it.

Inside was a green velvet blazer, beautifully lined in orange silk. She had tried it on at Jack's a week earlier but hadn't bought it, thinking it was too expensive—it had been hanging on the designer goods rack. She held it up under the porch light. She loved the blazer, but of course she couldn't say so.

"I saw you try it on," Devon confessed. "You looked so beautiful in it. I thought you should have it."

Haley struggled to keep the stern look on her face from melting into a gooey "aw." That had to be one of the sweetest things any boy had ever said to or done for her. But Irene's advice stayed with her, and she kept herself in check. "Thanks," she said in a flat voice. She granted him a vague smile—he'd bought her a present, after all—but that was it.

"So . . . you doing anything special tonight for your birthday?" Devon asked.

"I'll probably just go to the game or something," she said. The boys' varsity basketball team had a big game against their archrivals, Ridgewood, that night. It was the social event of the weekend in certain circles. Not in Devon's, of course, but he might have gone with Haley if she'd invited him. She didn't.

"Oh," he said. He paused a few seconds to give her one last chance to ask him along, but she didn't take it. "Well, happy birthday, Haley. See you around."

Haley went inside and closed the door before he'd even left the porch. Through the front window, she watched him walk away looking very dejected.

I'm doing everything you told me, Irene, she thought. *This better be worth it.*

• • •

If you think Irene's advice is genius and that Haley should stick with the plan and not let up on poor Devon, go to page 238, DESPERATELY SEEKING HALEY. If you think Devon's had enough, that his goose is

cooked and it's time for Haley to take him off the coals and reel him, go to page 243, IGNORE IRENE'S ADVICE. Finally, maybe Haley really is bored with Devon now and wants to go to Reese's basketball game on page 266, HOME GAME.

CANDLELIT BIRTHDAY

If the way to a man's heart is through his stomach, why shouldn't the same rule apply to girls?

It hit Haley as soon as Alex answered the door—a wonderful smell. A warm, homey, wintry supper smell that was far more decadent than anything wafting around the Millers' mostly vegetarian kitchen.

"Come in, come in." Alex looked adorable in a button-down shirt and tie covered by an apron. He led Haley into his family's traditional colonial house. The foyer was lit only by large candles scattered around on tabletops and lining each step up to the second floor. The rest of the Martin family was out of town, so the house was quiet except for some soft music playing on the stereo. They walked through the living room, where a fire roared in the fireplace. Then Alex led Haley into the dining room, where he had set the table beautifully. He'd used what was clearly his mother's best china and silver, which gleamed in the light of tall candles burning in a pair of silver candelabra.

"What smells so good?" Haley asked as she followed him into the kitchen. They were barely able to keep their hands off each other and seemed to have a physical need to be touching at all times. Pots simmered on the stove and something was roasting in the oven as Alex resumed chopping and stirring and sautéing.

"That would be steak au poivre, scalloped potatoes and sautéed spinach," Alex said. "I hope everything turns out okay. I don't exactly have a lot of experience cooking."

Haley was touched. Alex had clearly gone to a lot of trouble to make her birthday dinner perfect. She wondered if any of the other boys she knew would ever make this much effort to please her. Probably not.

Alex handed Haley a glass of sparkling cider. "Before we sit down to eat, I'd like to make a toast. Happy Valentine's Day, Haley, and happy birthday." Alex leaned over and kissed her passionately. Haley felt light-headed, pleasantly warm and as if her feet were no longer touching the floor. She was suddenly glad she'd remembered to shave her legs and put on the one pair of ecru lace underwear she owned.

"Thank you." Haley giggled. "And here's to your first steak au poivre." They sipped their cider.

It was all so sophisticated and grown up, but it also felt entirely natural being with Alex this way, alone in the house fixing dinner. Even though Haley had just been dropped off by her dad like a little girl.

Haley would have driven herself to Alex's house—she had, after all, passed her driver's test that afternoon and finally gotten her license, as well as a car of her very own. The problem was just that—her new car. Haley wasn't ready to introduce it to the world, not even to Alex.

Instead of coming home to a shiny new automobile in her driveway, Haley had driven up to find the large, pale yellow Lemon waiting for her—the battered and bruised sedan that had once belonged to her grandmother Polly. It was pretty much the ugliest car Haley had ever seen. It backfired like a cannon and was covered with bumper stickers like "I Brake for Cookies," "Lady in a Walker on Board" and "Sunday Drivers = Safe Drivers."

So, Haley told her parents a little white lie—that she wasn't comfortable driving by herself at night yet. Her father, predictably, thought Haley was being very mature and safety-minded, and said he'd be glad to drop her off. In fact, he told her to add an extra half hour to her curfew.

Alex opened the oven and checked on the potatoes. "I think we're ready. Go make yourself comfortable in the dining room, and I'll be right in."

Haley sat down at the candlelit table and put her napkin in her lap. Alex brought in the scalloped potatoes and the platter of spinach, followed by the steaks, dripping with a buttery pepper sauce. He served Haley first, then himself, and sat down.

"Delicious," she declared after taking her first bite, and it really was. She tried the vegetables, and they were wonderfully tender and flavorful too. "Everything is sooooo good," she moaned.

"Thank goodness," Alex said. "I didn't know what I'd do if it turned out badly. I'd hate to have to order emergency pizza for your birthday. That would not have been the memorable evening I was hoping for."

Haley laughed. "I wouldn't have minded. But this really is great." She paused for a sip of water. "So how are things different over at the governor's mansion now that Mrs. Eton's been officially sworn in?"

"Not any different, really, but even more intense, if that's possible," Alex said. "She's very focused on bringing more young people into the Republican Party, so guess who her point man is?"

"Spencer?" Haley said, laughing. "Sorry, I meant that as a joke."

"Yeah, Spencer isn't exactly a shining example of Republican virtue," Alex said. "Unfortunately, Mrs. Eton seems to think I have some kind of ability to control him. Believe me, Spencer does what he wants. He doesn't care what anyone says."

"Oh, I believe you." Haley spooned a little more potato onto her plate. The food was really outstanding. She was amazed that this was the first time Alex had prepared any of these dishes. But then again, he seemed to excel effortlessly at everything he tried.

They talked easily as they finished eating, about school and politics and life. Then Alex cleared away the plates and brought out a heart-shaped chocolate cake with seventeen candles on it for dessert. "Happy birthday, valentine," he said. Haley made a wish and blew out the candles. Then Alex leaned over and dropped a small velvet box into her lap.

"What's this?" Haley asked.

"A little something for the birthday girl. Or for Valentine's Day, whichever way you want to look at it. Open it."

Haley opened the box. Inside was a beautiful necklace: a sizeable gold heart dangling from a delicate chain. "Oh, Alex," she said. "I love it!"

"Let me put it on you." Alex stood up and draped the necklace over Haley's throat. As he did so, he his fingers to delicately trace the curve of her ,he turned to show him how it looked on her.

ι looks beautiful," he said. "And so do you." He ·d forward and kissed her again, more urgently this time. Haley kissed him back and melted into his arms.

"This is by far the most romantic Valentine's Day I've ever had," she murmured.

"Me too," Alex said. He touched her hair and ran his hands down the sides of her body. She shivered. They kissed again. "And it doesn't have to end yet."

"No?" Haley asked tentatively.

"We could go upstairs and have our dessert in my room." Alex let his hand travel down between Haley's thighs. She gasped a little, tantalized by Alex's touch, but also concerned that if she made her way upstairs, she might not make it home in time for curfew.

Then again, Annie had invited her to spend the night out. Maybe she could just call her parents and tell them she'd decided to sleep over at the Armstrongs'? That way, she and Alex could be alone all night. The more Alex caressed her, the more that started to seem like the best and only option.

• • •

Alex is really making a play for Haley, and he's certainly a catch—sweet, thoughtful and above all, smart. Next year, he'll be away at college, where coeds are sure to be throwing themselves at him. So what should Haley do?

If you think she's dying to go upstairs for a Valentine's Day hookup with Alex, to make sure he doesn't forget her after he goes away to school, go to page 250, SLEEP OVER. If you think she shouldn't rush things, and that it's important she doesn't abuse her parents' trust, go to page 257, MAKE CURFEW.

Once things progress to the bedroom, it can be difficult to slow down the momentum. You'd better make sure Haley is ready to go all the way—or do everything but—before she says yes and follows Alex upstairs.

Some people just don't like surprises.

After school on Haley's birthday, her dad picked her up and drove her to the DMV. There, she took her driver's test and passed with flying colors. She was a little shaky on three-point turns, but the woman scoring her road test didn't seem to pick up on it. Afterward, Haley ran outside to the waiting room and waved her brand-new driver's license at her dad.

"Congratulations!" He gave her a big hug. "My little girl's a driver. Want to chauffeur me home?"

Haley carefully maneuvered her parents' hybrid

from the DMV for the twenty blocks or so to her own street. She was beginning to feel comfortable behind the wheel when, right as she turned into her driveway, she nearly rear-ended a hideous car that was blocking the garage. It was a large, pale yellow sedan covered with bumper stickers like "I Brake for Cookies," "Lady in a Walker on Board" and "Sunday Drivers = Safe Drivers." Haley recognized it instantly as her grandmother's old Lemon, famous for the way it backfired every few feet.

"Is Gam Polly here for my birthday?" Haley asked enthusiastically. "If that's the case, I'll forgive her for parking her giant monstrosity of a car in my parking space."

"That giant monstrosity . . . is your new car!" Perry announced. "Happy seventeenth birthday, Snoodles!"

"What?" Haley was stunned. She'd been hoping for a car—a new car. Barring that, she'd been hoping for something she wouldn't be too embarrassed to be seen in. But this—this was a travesty. Her worst nightmare, on wheels. "You say that like it's a good thing."

Her father laughed. "It's all yours, Haley. You deserve it."

You mean I deserve to be punished? she thought. *Because that's what this feels like.*

"Yay," she said halfheartedly, purely for her father's benefit.

Her birthday dinner with the family that night cheered her up a little. Haley knew she shouldn't sulk about getting Gam Polly's clunker instead of a cool new ride, like the one Coco got on her birthday or even Annie Armstrong's tiny electric car. She supposed the Lemon was better than no car at all, and she tried to be a good sport about it.

However, she absolutely refused to drive the car to the game that night. She wasn't ready to introduce the Lemon to the world, and she doubted she ever would be. What would Coco say if she saw Haley driving an old-lady car? What would any of her friends think?

Haley didn't want to know. Besides, she figured, if she didn't have a car, she would need a ride home. And maybe that would give her an excuse to approach Reese Highland, her handsome—and lately estranged—neighbor. So she told her parents she didn't feel ready to drive alone at night yet, and they happily agreed to drop her off at school for the game.

Haley slipped into the gym in the middle of the first quarter. During their on-again moments, Reese had told Haley many times over that he had one rule about game days: no surprises. He loved having Haley in the crowd, so long as he was prepared to see her there. But he hated the idea of her showing up at a game unexpectedly—it threw off his timing.

However, Haley just assumed all those silly rules were out the window now that they were no longer doing anything close to dating. After all, she'd barely spoken to Reese since he'd returned from his winter trip to Nevis with Spencer and the guys. Reese had been caught on camera snuggling up to a swimsuit model, and after that, Haley had barely given him the time of day.

Lately, though, she'd been hearing talk that Reese had been set up by Spencer and the gang on the trip. Apparently, they had spiked his drink and then encouraged one of the girls to cozy up to him. In his inebriated state, Reese hadn't been able to protest. In fact, he was so out of it he'd barely known what was going on.

Now all Haley wanted was to have him back in her life, even if that meant just being friends for a while. This game was huge for Reese—Hillsdale was battling it out with Ridgewood, their eternal rival, for first place in the division. The only bigger game would be the following week when Hillsdale went to Ridgewood for a rematch in the play-offs. Haley innocently hoped a show of support would go a long way toward making amends. Wouldn't he notice if she didn't bother to show up at all for his big game? Wouldn't that, more than anything, make the distance between them grow? That was Haley's line of thinking, anyway, as she sat down in the bleachers, blending into the crowd.

At first Reese was too busy playing to notice her, and he played a great first half. He scored sixteen points and logged five assists. By halftime the Hawks were up by three. The game was close but Hillsdale was always a step ahead of their rivals.

Haley cheered along with the crowd but didn't do anything to draw attention to herself. Then, early in the second half, a Ridgewood player fouled Reese. As he stepped up to the line to take his foul shot—his specialty—Haley couldn't resist calling out, "Go, Reese!" breaking the silence in the crowded gym. Reese heard her and looked toward her, distracted. He caught her eye and looked wounded, surprised. Her heart sank. *Uh-oh.* She knew she had made a terrible mistake, not calling first to warn him of her presence.

Reese bounced the ball, trying to regain his concentration. He took his first foul shot—missed. The crowd groaned. Second shot—missed again. Not like Reese at all. Haley wanted to sink under the bleachers and hide.

After that, Reese's game went further downhill. He missed another foul shot and, most embarrassing of all, he completely blew three wide-open layups. He didn't score another point for the rest of the game. Reese Highland, star hoops player, looked like a klutz out there on the court. His teammates tried to pick up the slack but it wasn't enough. Ridgewood took advantage and surged past the Hawks. Final score: 68 to 53, Ridgewood. The Hawks had suffered a humiliating meltdown.

Devastated, the crowd booed the team off the court. As the spectators dispersed, Haley heard them muttering things like "What a joke" and "What happened to Highland? He completely lost it out there."

"He played like my grandmother after she's had a few scotches," one guy said. "And that ain't good."

Haley felt terrible. She'd meant well. She'd only wanted to support him. Had this big loss really been all her fault?

Maybe Reese will forgive me, she thought. *Our relationship is more important than a basketball game, right?* She clung to that thin thread of hope even as, deep down, she had her doubts. Strong doubts.

Still in denial, Haley waited for Reese to emerge from the locker room. It took a long time. All the other players came out first, wet-headed and dejected, and left with barely a glance in Haley's direction. At last, Reese came out and headed straight for his car.

"Reese!" Haley called. "Wait!"

He kept walking and didn't look back.

"Reese!" She ran up and tugged on his arm. He shrugged her off, then turned to face her.

"Haley, you haven't even spoken to me in weeks, and then you show up here tonight without telling me? When the one thing I've ever asked you not to do is surprise me during a game? There were easier ways of getting my attention."

She shrank back, startled. He'd never spoken to

her so harshly before. "I—I just wanted to say I'm sorry. About the game. About everything. I should have given you a chance to explain after . . . Nevis."

"Yes, you should have," Reese said. "But you clearly don't trust me or have any respect for our relationship."

"Of course I do, Reese," Haley said. "That's why I came. I wanted to show you how much I care about—"

"It's too late," he said, sounding truly disappointed. "I can't listen to this right now." He got into his car and started the engine. And Haley was left in the parking lot without a ride home—and without a boyfriend.

• • •

Haley should have known better. After all that's happened between her and Reese, and after she saw those very suggestive pictures from Nevis, she should have picked a quieter and more private place to talk things out, rather than surprising him in the middle of a crucial game.

Go back to page 1.

DEAD END

CONFRONT COCO

Talking sense into a girl on a diet is roughly equivalent to snatching food from a hungry lion.

Haley's hand twitched from nerves as she rang the doorbell at Coco's enormous McMansion. Haley had grown increasingly worried about her friend in recent days. Lately, Coco had appeared to be eating nothing at all—or at least not anything beyond a couple of orange slices, some green tea and a hot water/lemon juice/cayenne pepper/dash of maple syrup concoction. The extreme fad dieting had allowed her to shrink from skinny to superskinny in under two weeks, though Coco had also apparently had help from a slew of dangerous diet pills. Haley had caught her popping a handful at school earlier that day.

Haley had considered reporting Coco to the school nurse for treatment. But then she pictured Coco's likely response: threats, screams, all-out warfare. She thought better of that idea, deciding instead to have a heart-to-heart with Coco at her house, on her home turf, where she'd be most comfortable.

Coco's maid, Consuela, answered the door. "'Ello Meez 'Aley," she said. "You want to see Meez Coco? She upstairs in her room."

"Thank you, Consuela." Haley started up the steps to Coco's bedroom, surprised to have gotten by the first line of defense so easily. *Things must have loosened up in the De Clerq household,* she thought. Coco usually consigned Consuela to be a bouncer and protect her from unwanted guests. Haley had never before been allowed simply to run up to Coco's room uninvited and unannounced. This was most definitely a first.

Coco's door was ajar. Haley knocked and Coco called, "Come in." She looked surprised to see Haley but not displeased. She was lounging on her daybed, reading a book about the deplorable conditions at most livestock farms, which Haley recognized since her mother owned at least two copies.

"Every time I start craving a steak, I just read a chapter about hormone injections or cattle pens," Coco explained. "Kills the appetite, let me tell you."

"Speaking of eating," Haley said, making herself comfortable in one of Coco's overstuffed chairs. "I wanted to talk to you about your cleanse."

"It's great, isn't it?" Coco touched one of her cheeks. "Look what it's done for my skin."

"Your skin does look great," Haley said. "But then, it always did. It's your bones I'm worried about."

"Ugh, not you too?" Coco said with a sigh of exasperation. "Please don't try to talk some sense into me, Haley. It won't work."

"Coco, you must have lost at least ten pounds. And you were a thin girl to begin with. Do you know how much damage you can do, to your heart, your kidneys, your skeletal system? Starvation diets can lead to heart failure, osteoporosis, death!"

"I've only lost nine and a half pounds, actually," Coco said, ignoring Haley's warnings. "Ten is my goal, then I'll stop." But Haley wasn't so sure.

"Lots of girls can't stop," Haley pressed on, "once they begin starving themselves. Look at all the problems Whitney had with her binging and purging. It took *a lot* of couseling to get her straightened out. And you know how she follows you around and copies your every move. If only for Whitney's sake, you should take better care of yourself."

"Huh, Whitney," Coco huffed. "She has no self-control at all, no willpower. Do you think she's maintained the cleanse? Of course not. Her mother has her eating salads and leafy greens the minute she walks in the door after school."

"Thank goodness," Haley muttered, glad to know at least Whitney wasn't endangering herself.

"Look, Haley, it's not as bad as you think. I like my body. I liked it before I started dieting. I have no interest in starving or exercising myself into oblivion. I'm taking in plenty of calories, I swear. I've even been keeping a log." Coco pulled out a little black book, with dates from the previous two weeks and lists of ingested—albeit liquid—items that added up to nine hundred calories a day.

"What about those diet pills I saw you swallowing by the handful?"

"Those are just little herbal pick-me-ups from my trainer," Coco said. "One hundred percent natural. And if you don't believe me, you can ask him yourself." Coco held out her cell phone, which Haley refused to take. "This is all just to get back at Spencer," Coco continued. "To make him eat his heart out. I know I always looked great, but this winter I want to get down to my 'sucks for you' weight."

"'Sucks for you'?"

"You know—the pound-to-muscle-mass ratio that guarantees every girl at school wants to be me, every guy wants to bed me and Spencer's brain implodes at the sight of me doing my runway sashay through the halls. It's not a body-image thing—it's a power thing. Come on, Haley. I'm only half a pound away from my target, and then I'll give up the herbal supplements for good. Promise."

Haley felt reasonably reassured. "Okay," she said. "But I'm giving you three more days, and after that, if I catch you popping any more pills, supplements or otherwise, I'm calling Nurse Underhill and then I'm calling your parents."

Haley left the house believing she had accomplished something and feeling proud of herself for her efforts. However, that feeling was not to last. By the time she got home, she had several texts on her phone from Whitney, Sasha and Cecily. Coco, in her effort to shed that final half pound in the three days Haley had allotted her, had immediately popped three more "pick-me-ups" and called an emergency session with her Pilates instructor.

It turned into an emergency session, all right. Coco's heart rate soared, and her teacher, fearing Coco might be having some sort of cardiac event, called 911. Coco was rushed to the hospital and kept for observation for three days. Her doctors determined that the pills she'd been popping were basically a knockoff of the outlawed diet drug fenphen.

So much for those herbal supplements.

• • •

Looks as though Haley should have gone straight to Nurse Underhill. Coco could have been in serious

trouble, no thanks to Haley. Dieting is one thing; popping pills of unknown origin is another. Haley should have known better than to assume Coco was in control of the situation.

Hang your head and go back to page 1.

DEAD END

CALL THE NURSE

Sometimes reinforcements are required.

Haley hesitated on the threshold of Ms. Underhill's office. She was worried about Coco, who seemed to be eating nothing more than orange segments, green tea and some kind of crazy cleanse concoction that was mostly hot water with a dash of cayenne pepper, lemon juice and a splash of maple syrup. Coco had shrunk from skinny to superskinny in two weeks, and Haley was beginning to worry that she might have an eating disorder, especially since she'd recently caught Coco popping pills of unknown origin.

But what could Haley do about it? She didn't really know, but Ms. Underhill, the school nurse, had recently talked to the school about her concerns over the terrible eating habits that were sweeping through the student body. She seemed to know a lot about the subject. She was a medical professional, after all. Still, nobody took pleasure in visiting Ms. Underhill. And Haley was nervous about how Coco would react when she discovered Haley had been the one to turn her in. Luckily, she'd brought along Sasha for moral support.

Haley took a breath, and she and Sasha walked into Nurse Underhill's office. "What is it?" Ms. Underhill asked, her manner more drill sergeant than nurse.

"We're sorry to bother you—" Haley began.

"You're not bothering me!" Ms. Underhill shouted. "I'm here to help!"

Haley found the disconnect between Ms. Underhill's helpful words and stern manner confusing, but she plowed ahead. "We're worried about a friend of ours. We don't know for sure, but we think she might have an eating problem."

"Haley caught her popping diet pills in the lunchroom," Sasha blurted out.

Ms. Underhill frowned and grabbed a clipboard and pen. "Name?"

"My name? Haley Miller."

"No, name of the problem eater."

"Oh. Coco De Clerq."

"Yes, I know the girl." Ms. Underhill wrote down Coco's name. "You very well could be right. What other kinds of behavior have you observed?"

"Behavior?" Haley hadn't expected this question. Did Nurse Underhill expect them to whip out a log? "Well, we just never see her eating anything, not any solid food anyway. For the past two weeks, she hasn't been eating breakfast, lunch or dinner, just the occasional orange segment, or green tea, or this cleansing water. . . ."

"Let me guess," said Nurse Underhill. "It's made with hot water, cayenne pepper, lemon juice and maple syrup."

"You know the recipe," Sasha confirmed.

"She's clearly dropping weight. I would say close to ten pounds in ten days," said Haley.

"That's good enough for me." Ms. Underhill slapped the clipboard down on her desk. "Thank you, Haley and Sasha. You did the right thing. We'll get Coco the help she needs." She clicked through her computer files until she found Coco's contact information. "I'm calling Principal Crum. We're going to get in touch with Miss De Clerq's parents."

"Um, I think Coco's parents are in St. Barts," Sasha chimed in.

Ms. Underhill raised an eyebrow. "Really? All the more reason to bring them back from their little paradise vacation and force them to take a good look at how much their daughter is suffering."

Yikes, Haley thought. *That's only going to make Coco more pissed when she finds out who spoke up.*

"Nurse Underhill," Sasha said, "this is all confidential, right? I mean, Coco's never going to know who told you she was in trouble, right?"

"Of course!" Nurse Underhill boomed.

And all Haley could say was, "Why didn't I think of that?"

• • •

Thank goodness Haley and Sasha went to Nurse Underhill. Now the problem is out of their hands, and Coco will be strictly monitored to make sure she's getting enough to eat. And if they're lucky, Coco will never know that it was Haley and Sasha who turned her in. Haley can take a deep breath and move on.

Go straight to MUSICAL VALENTINE on page 227.

MUSICAL VALENTINE

If revenge is best served cold, February is a good time for it.

"Guess what I just heard?" Coco said with glee as she snapped her cell phone shut. She had gathered the girls—Haley, Sasha, Whitney and Cecily—at Bubbies Bistro for a game-night/Valentine's Day protest dinner. Well, that and to mark Haley's seventeenth birthday. They were just collecting the check when Coco got a text from one of her underclassman minions. "Ridgewood destroyed Hillsdale tonight! Ha! I knew those boys were losers."

The girls clasped their gloved hands to celebrate.

Four of their ex-boyfriends—Reese, Spencer, Johnny and Drew—were the stars of Hillsdale's basketball team, and that night's matchup against archrival Ridgewood was the most important game of the season. As far as the girls were concerned, the boys deserved to be humiliated on the court after their R-rated Caribbean vacation, during which they were photographed hanging all over a group of scantily clad swimsuit models.

That afternoon, Haley had taken her driver's test and fortunately passed with flying colors. Unfortunately, her parents had given her a car, and not just any car: they expected her to drive her grandmother Polly's hideous, backfiring, pale yellow beast of a sedan, nicknamed the Lemon. It had white Naugahyde seats and was covered with bumper stickers like "I Brake for Cookies," "Lady in a Walker on Board" and "Sunday Drivers = Safe Drivers." Nothing on the road was more unfortunate.

Haley had been hoping for a car—but a shiny new car. Barring that, she at least wanted something she wouldn't be embarrassed to be seen in. No such luck. She hid the Lemon in the garage and vowed never to let it out. And after telling her parents she still didn't feel comfortable driving after dark, she hitched a ride to Bubbies with Sasha.

Coco had called for skipping the game and having a girls-only Valentine's Day to celebrate their "new year, new you" success. The girls had all been dieting and had never looked better, and Coco had just officially lifted the ban on solid foods. The fact that the boys had lost their big game only sweetened the night for them. It was as if the universe were punishing the boys for their bad behavior and rewarding all the girls—well, except for Haley. She was being punished with the Lemon.

"Serves them right," Sasha said.

"I bet they lost because they couldn't concentrate," Whitney said. "They were so devastated by being dumped by the four of you. You took their mojo!"

Out in the parking lot, Matthew Graham rolled up in his expensive European sedan, which was filled with rowdy, victorious Ridgewood basketball players. "Hey, girls," Matthew said suggestively. He was an old friend of Spencer's, though they sometimes had notorious falling-outs, and this was apparently one of those times. Matt and Spence had been at boarding school together once upon a time but both had been kicked out, and now Spencer was at Hillsdale, Matt at Ridgewood. "Tough loss. Want to skip the Hillsdale pity parties and kick it with some winners for a change?"

"What did you have in mind?" Coco asked.

"Big dance at Ridgewood tonight," Matt said. "Everybody's hopped up from the win. Come help us celebrate. You know it would burn Spencer if you came partying with us."

"Oh, Matthew," Coco said with a theatrical sigh. "What are you guys fighting about now?"

"He didn't invite me on his exclusive island getaway," Matt said. "I didn't care at first—he told me it was going to be a quiet family trip, and I have no interest in that. But when I saw the pictures, I took it as a personal affront that Spencer kept me away from those girls. So now that we've crushed him in basketball, I'd like to twist the knife by celebrating with the hottest girls from his school."

"Makes perfect sense to me," Coco said.

The girls gathered to consult. "If the boys hear we spent Valentine's Day with their worst enemies, it will kill them," Coco said. "I say we go to the dance."

"It would be a chance to meet some new boys," Whitney said, clapping her hands.

"And crush our cheating, lying, no-good exes' hearts even deeper into the dirt," Cecily said. "I love it."

"Let's show those guys they're not the only game in town," Sasha said. "We don't need them, right, Haley?"

Haley thought of how hurt she had felt when she saw the pictures of Reese and those models. Maybe this could help her heal. "I'm in," she said.

"Girls? The party is waiting," Matt said.

"We're coming," Coco told him.

"Great," he said. "Follow us."

The girls piled into Sasha's car and followed Matt

to Ridgewood High's Valentine's Day dance. Luckily they were already wearing flirty party dresses for their big night out at Bubbies. Ridgewood had a preppier vibe than Hillsdale, with boys in blue blazers over their jeans and girls in neat dresses.

"Welcome to Ridgewood, my lovelies," Matt said. "Have a drink."

He eyed the girls as he handed out plastic cups with some kind of pink liquid in them. Haley took a sip. She had no idea what it was, but knowing Matt, the drink probably contained at least one hundred-proof ingredient. After a few more sips, she started feeling suspiciously relaxed.

The girls lined up against the wall to survey the mysterious new crop of boys. "Not bad," Coco said, nodding at a tall blond basketball forward. He noticed her interest and came up to her. "Dance?" the blond asked Coco. She took his hand and let him lead her onto the dance floor. Cecily paired up with a very cute boy with brown hair that curled behind his ears. A buff point guard with a short Afro twirled Sasha onto the floor, while Haley found herself cornered by the notorious womanizer Matt.

"Hey there," he purred. "So Reese Highland's history, eh? I don't mind following in his footsteps. I always thought he had great taste."

Haley had to keep herself from wrinkling her nose in disgust. She was all for meeting new guys, but Matt Graham was hardly an unknown quantity—

and what she knew about him wasn't good. She had to admit he was cute, though—in the preppy Spencer mold, of course, only darker—and he could be charming when he wanted to be. The trouble was, he wanted to be charming for all the wrong reasons, like to get a girl drunk and separate her from her pants.

Three minutes into the dance Matt was running his hands down Haley's back. She was racking her brain for an excuse not to dance to another song with Mr. Paws when his eyes darted over to Whitney—or more specifically, Whitney's bursting cleavage. "Hel-lo," he said, turning away from Haley, but not before grabbing a friend and plunking him down in front of her as his replacement.

Matt's friend, a tall, blue-eyed cutie in glasses, smiled down at her. "Hi," he said.

"Hi," she said, relieved to be rid of Matt and glad to have a new prospect to dance with.

"My name's Rob," he said. "Feel like dancing?"

"Yes, in fact, I do." Haley took Rob's hand and they grooved to a hip-hop hit. Even though the song was fast and funky, Rob kept pulling Haley close and grinding up against her as if it were a ballad. She glanced around and noticed that her friends were being pawed in the same way. This preppy Ridgewood crew was a little more hands-on than the Hillsdale girls were used to, and harder to control. A subtle nudge away wasn't enough to keep the boys from coming back for more.

I guess it means he likes me, Haley told herself, but she didn't feel completely comfortable. Fortunately, she didn't have long to think about it, because she was soon caught up in a game of musical boys. Coco poached Cecily's cutie, so Cecily snagged Sasha's studly point guard, leaving Sasha eyeing Haley's Rob. Haley found herself passed from one boy to the next before she even had a chance to learn their names.

Finally, Haley somehow found herself stuck with the least attractive guy in the group. He was tall and a basketball player, but that didn't help. He had invisible braces that weren't invisible enough, horrible acne on his jutting chin, booze on his breath and a tendency to spit when he talked.

Just her luck, at that moment the DJ called for a slow dance. Haley sighed as Acne Boy took her in his arms. "I sweated so much at the game my chin broke out," Acne Boy said self-consciously. Haley shut her eyes so that he couldn't see her rolling them. Why did he feel the need to explain? Acne was acne; she didn't care how he got it. But talking about it definitely made it worse.

"It was worth it, though—it's worth anything to kick Reese Highland's butt. That guy's so stuck-up. Thinks he's so great because of his perfect skin."

That's true, Haley thought sadly. *Reese's skin*

never breaks out. She suddenly missed him very much.

The dance was winding down. "Some Valentine's Day, huh?" Acne Boy said. "There's an afterparty at the Morton place. It's just up the street."

They'd passed "the Morton place" on their way to the dance. It was a huge gated estate. Haley had no idea who lived there, but any party at an estate, especially when Matt Graham was involved, was bound to be lively, to say the least.

"I don't know," Haley said. "I've got to check with my friends."

She broke away from him and joined Coco and Company in a huddle. "We have to go to the afterparty," Coco said. "It will sweeten our revenge on the boys. We can take pictures of ourselves partying at this fabulous estate with these new guys and post them on the Internet to make sure we really rub it into the boys' faces."

"Do we have to stay with the boys we were dancing with?" Whitney asked. "Mine smells like vodka."

"No, we can keep switching around or whatever," Coco said. "Remember—girl power! We've got to stick together."

"So, you girls coming to the party?" Matt brazenly inserted himself into the circle and interrupted their deliberations. "It won't be the same without you."

"We're coming," Coco said. "Spencer and his friends are going to be so pissed when they hear about this."

Matt laughed. "I don't think so. I texted Spencer that I was bringing you girls to the dance, so it's not exactly going to shock them."

Coco's mouth fell open. "They know? What did Spencer say?"

"He seemed like he couldn't care less. I was surprised, to be honest. He said he and the boys were going to console themselves with a few freshman rally girls. I think he's throwing an impromptu SIGMA." SIGMA was an exclusive traveling party Spencer sometimes held, notorious for wild goings-on. Drinking, gambling, hooking up . . . it all happened at a SIGMA party, and whenever Spencer threw one, it was always the place to be. Suddenly the school gym at Ridgewood High seemed dull and dreary by comparison, in spite of all the elaborate Valentine's Day decorations.

Coco looked like a volcano about to erupt. Her plan had backfired horribly. The Ridgewood boys who'd seemed so cute only minutes before—well, except for Haley's dance partner—now looked like big dorky goons who couldn't keep their hands to themselves. Coco had been had, and she wasn't taking it well.

"We're out!" she commanded. She marched out of the gym. Haley followed her, thrilled to leave Acne Boy behind.

"What a rip," Whitney muttered when they were outside on the sidewalk in front of the school. "We wasted our whole Valentine's Day on those Ridgewood dorks!"

"Yeah, if I wanted to dance with someone who had two left feet I could have stayed home and boogied with my dad," Cecily said.

"Let's get out of here," Sasha said.

They started for Sasha's car, but Haley held back a little. It was her birthday, after all, and so far she hadn't had much fun. She wished she could go somewhere else before the night was over and have at least a little adventure.

"Come on, Haley," Coco called from Sasha's car.

Just then a blue sports car pulled up and stopped in front of Haley. "Hey, going to the party or what?" It was Rob, Mr. Glasses with the sweet blue eyes—the cutest one of Matt's friends. Haley paused, considering what she should do.

• • •

Well, that was a bust. Coco's plan totally backfired. If the girls want another chance to take revenge on their hoop-shooting exes, they'll have to think of something better than flirting with the boys from Ridgewood. The girls wasted the evening fending off handsy jocks they don't even like. Except for Mr. Glasses, that is—he could be different. Who knows? Anything's possible. Haley barely knows the guy, but if she doesn't give him a

chance, she never will. And how does she know he won't turn out to be the love of her life?

If you think Haley should give adventure one more shot before her birthday night is over, have her get into the car with Mr. Glasses on page 261, DATE WITH DWI. If you're looking forward to seeing Hillsdale take on Ridgewood in a play-offs rematch, go to HOME GAME on page 266.

It's Valentine's Day, and you get only one of those a year. It's not very romantic unless you have a valentine to celebrate with. But will any old valentine do? That's up to you.

DESPERATELY SEEKING HALEY

Sometimes playing hard to get really works.

Haley felt a little down. It was the day after her birthday, the day after Valentine's Day, and nothing had really changed. She woke up that morning and thought, *I'm seventeen,* and she felt happy, but what did it really mean? Was anything different? Nothing she could point to. Sure, she had her driver's license now, but her new car was so heinous she didn't want to be seen in it. What good was having your license if you didn't even want to drive?

Then, that afternoon, the doorbell rang. It was Devon. He looked terrible: more rumpled than usual, with circles under his eyes as if he hadn't slept well or was under a lot of stress.

"Haley, I need to talk to you," he announced.

Haley wasn't eager to let him inside—her parents and Mitchell were home, and they were all pretty nosy. The air was crisp but the afternoon sun warmed the front steps, so Haley sat down with Devon outside.

"What's up?" He looked so distraught she automatically softened the cold manner she'd been using with him lately. On Irene's advice she'd been basically ignoring him, but she didn't have the nerve to go hard-core on him just then.

He poured his heart out. "I—I've just got to come out and say it: you're the most amazing girl I've ever met. I made a huge mistake not telling you this sooner. And getting mixed up with Darcy, who I realized I don't even like. But you! You, I totally and completely adore you, Haley. I think I might be falling in love."

Haley stared at him in amazement. Was this really Devon? Telling her he adored her? That he thought he was in love? She'd been waiting for this day for so long, and now that it was finally here she felt as if she needed to pinch herself.

"I've always adored you," he continued. "But I

guess I was too afraid to say anything. Or I didn't realize it, maybe. You know, I can't always read you. You're so confusing!"

Inside, Haley wanted to laugh. *She* was confusing? Look who was talking!

"Sometimes I think you like me, and sometimes I think you don't know I'm alive," Devon said. "I just can't tell. And we have such a cool friendship, and I'd never want to mess it up. I've been crazy about you for ages but I was afraid if I told you and you didn't feel the same way our friendship would be ruined."

He paused to look at her, to gauge her reaction. Haley didn't know what to do. Should she drop the cold act? It had almost become second nature to her by now. Or should she keep him dangling and see how far he would go?

She nodded, staying neutral for now. He kept talking.

"Lately I've realized that what I feel for you is really serious. I realized I had to say something to you or risk losing the most amazing, inspiring person in my life. You're so beautiful and smart and funny, and so cool, and you're graceful and have this great style and you're nice to people . . . you have a good heart . . . you're really everything, Haley."

Her heart was pounding. This was one of the most beautiful, heartfelt speeches a boy had ever made to her. She'd been longing to hear someone say something like this ever since she could remember.

She just never thought that someone would be Devon. This was a total shocker.

"I don't know why I'm telling you this," Devon said, his head sinking as he still got no reaction from her. "It's a total waste of time. Next year you'll get into some incredible college and go away and forget all about me. And I'll—well, who knows if I'll even be able to afford to go to college. I'll be some townie schlub and you'll be a fancy college girl. Once you start dating rich Ivy League guys you'll look back and remember Hillsdale as small-time. You won't think of me the same way anymore. You and your college friends will probably laugh over the rinky-dink high school boys you once knew. Ha-ha, that jerk Devon."

Haley was stunned. She truly didn't know what to say. She'd gotten her wish, all right. Devon was out-of-control, crazy in love with her. The question was, what should she do now?

• • •

That Irene Chen is an evil genius. She should write her own advice column! She pegged Devon perfectly and her instructions for Haley couldn't have worked better.

But now Haley has the upper hand, and with power comes responsibility. Devon has basically dropped his heart at her feet and said, *Do with it what you will. Pick it up or stomp on it.* That's a lot of pressure for young Haley.

What do you think she should do? If you think she should stick with Irene's plan and keep Devon dangling on the line as long as possible, turn to page 274, DARK VICTORY. If you think she's had enough adoration and it's time to level with Devon and be brutally honest, go to page 279, SLOPPY SECONDS.

Devon has bared his soul to Haley, but is that what she wanted? Didn't she just want him to pay a little attention to her? Perhaps you think naked souls turn Haley off. Perhaps Devon's big confession strikes her as just the teensiest bit juvenile after his escapades with Darcy, and Haley would just as soon write him off. If you think she would like to forget about Devon altogether and see what college boys are really like, head up to visit Coco's sister at Yale on page 288, SPRING BREAK AT YALE.

IGNORE IRENE'S ADVICE

Listening to your heart can lead you down a dark alley to nowhere.

On the Monday after her birthday Haley wore her new blazer—the beautiful green velvet one with the orange lining that Devon had given her—to school. When she walked into art class her eyes went straight to Devon, who was sitting alone at the pottery wheel. She flashed him a warm smile and touched the jacket to make sure he got the message: she liked it, and him, very much.

Irene had warned her not to let Devon know how much he meant to her, to put it off as long as she could. And Irene's advice had worked beautifully so far. Devon was practically groveling at Haley's feet. Once he gave her the jacket—a birthday gift that he'd sweetly noticed she liked—Haley figured it was time to stop playing games. He'd made his feelings very clear. Wasn't it time to let him off the hook? Haley couldn't stand pretending to be cold to him another second.

She walked across the room and sat beside him. He grinned happily at her. This was great—all Haley's dreams finally come true.

"I love the jacket," she said. "I just wanted to make sure you knew that. It was such a sweet and thoughtful gift."

His smile faded. "It's no big deal," he said. "Just an old jacket from work. It's not like I paid for it or anything."

Haley felt the chill instantly. *What just happened?* she thought. All she said was that she liked the gift he had given her. Was that one little thank-you enough to cool his feelings for her so quickly?

Without another glance at her, he dipped his hand into a bag of clay and plopped a gooey gray blob onto the potter's wheel. He was withdrawing, and fast.

I've got to do something, Haley thought. She knew he liked her—she *knew* it. All her instincts told her to move in fast and seal the deal with him before he pulled away completely.

"What are you going to make?" she asked, nodding at the clay on the wheel.

"A pot. What do you think?" Devon replied stiffly.

Mr. Von, the art teacher, called for class to start. Haley moved away to work on her own project, a collage of ice and other frozen objects. She'd started it to inspire her to keep cool with Devon. Now she felt like trashing it.

You won't slip away from me now, she thought with a glance at Devon, who slumped morosely over his clay, refusing to look up. *Not when I've gotten so close.*

Now that she'd had a taste of Devon's affection, she wanted more. She wanted all of him.

She caught up to him in the parking lot after school that day. "Devon!" she called, chasing after him. "Want to go to a movie or something later?"

He gaped at her as if he didn't quite remember who she was. *How can he switch gears so suddenly?* she wondered. Only a few days earlier he was begging her to go to a photography show with him. Now he just stared at his boots and said, "A movie? Uh, no, thanks. I can't."

"Maybe over the weekend, then?" She could hear herself pushing him, hear Irene screaming at her to stop, but she couldn't help herself.

"Yeah, maybe," he said. "I'll call you."

She skipped away, satisfied for the moment. He'd

said they could get together that weekend. Maybe. He'd call her.

Well, she waited all weekend for him to call, but the phone stayed quiet. *I guess he's just busy,* she told herself. *Or maybe he'll call later, at the last minute.* Devon could often be spontaneous that way.

She decided to distract herself by going out for some coffee. She had her cell with her in case Devon called. She stopped in at Drip for a latte to go. While she was waiting she spotted Devon at a table in the corner by the stage. She started to wave hello to him but stopped when she saw who he was with: Darcy.

Not her again, Haley thought, her heart sinking. She'd thought she'd gotten Darcy out of the way. So that was how Devon was spending the weekend. Well, if he had plans, why didn't he just say so? Why did he tell her he'd call if he never meant to?

He did mean to, Haley told herself. *Darcy is probably distracting him on purpose. She saw how much he started liking me and is hanging around him as much as she can to win him back. Well, it won't work,* Haley vowed. *He's mine. I'll show her.*

Her latte arrived. She took the cup and walked over to Devon's table. He and Darcy were laughing about something, and Darcy was pawing him as usual.

"Devon. Hi," Haley said. "What a surprise to see you here."

Devon did seem surprised to see her, but not pleasantly so. "Oh. Hey, Haley."

Darcy didn't bother saying hello. Haley decided to ignore her too. "So, are we going to a movie later or what?" Haley said.

"Sorry, Haley, he's busy," Darcy said.

"I think he can speak for himself, can't you, Devon?" Haley said.

"Darcy's right. I am busy," he said. "Sorry."

"I thought you said we would do something this weekend," Haley said.

"I never said that. I said maybe. I said we'd talk about it."

"You said you'd call me," Haley said. She held up her phone. "I don't see your number here under Recent Calls."

"I was going to call you—if you'd just give me a chance. . . ."

Haley could feel that she was pushing too hard. She decided to let it go—this time. He was obviously under the pernicious influence of the evil Darcy. It wasn't his fault.

"No worries," she said, trying to sound more lighthearted than she felt. "I just didn't want to let you down if you were looking forward to seeing me, that's all."

Darcy stifled a laugh. Devon said, "Oh. Thanks. I think I'll be okay."

Haley left with her latte, her cheeks burning. It was all Darcy's fault! Why did that little peroxide blonde have so much sway over Devon? It had to stop. That was all there was to it.

The rest of the week Haley trailed Devon wherever he went. If she saw him in the cafeteria, she sat with him, no matter who else was there. She started working with clay in art class so that she could use the pottery wheel next to his. She texted him after school, just asking what he was up to. But the more she chased him, the faster he ran away. Haley didn't get it. What was she doing wrong?

Then one day she walked into school and saw Devon from behind, wearing a new T-shirt. He had access to a silk-screening machine at Jack's, and he often used it to make his own shirts.

"Devon!" She ran up to him. "You made a new shirt. What's it say?"

He turned around. Across his chest, in metallic silver letters, was the word *Stalker*. He looked at her sheepishly. He wasn't a mean guy; he didn't set out to hurt people's feelings. But Haley took one look at that shirt and knew that the message was aimed straight at her.

He thought of her as a stalker now. Things had changed so much in just a few days.

"Huh. Funny," she said. She walked away, defeated.

I give up, she thought. She knew now that she

had somehow let herself get obsessed with Devon, all the while thinking he was the one obsessed with her. She was totally humiliated. But she wasn't so obsessed that she didn't know when to stop when the truth slapped her in the face.

She should have stuck with Irene's plan, she realized. It had been working so well, and she'd ruined everything by ignoring Irene's wisdom.

I lost control, Haley realized. *Devon wins.*

Worse yet, Darcy wins.

• • •

Haley really blew it this time. She made a complete fool of herself, chasing after Devon that way. Who knew Irene was such a fount of wisdom about boys? In Devon's case, at least, she knew what she was talking about. Haley should have heeded her advice.

Now Darcy has Devon all to herself, and Haley feels like an idiot. Next time, listen to Irene.

Hang your head and go back to page 1.

DEAD END

SLEEP OVER

If your mom is a lawyer with an investigative bent, it's probably not so smart to lie to her.

Alex had already prepared for this moment: he'd covered every empty surface in his room with candles. As he lit them, Haley looked around. She was relieved to see that his room was not the still-clearly-a-little-boy's-room that so many guys her age had. No sports car bedspread, no band posters on the wall, no toy dinosaurs strewn across the floor. It was neat and tidy, as she expected Alex's room would be, but also warm and masculine and mature. The bedspread was plaid, the furniture antique pine, the walls a tasteful shade of hunter green. And the bed, Haley couldn't help but notice, was a double, not a twin.

Alex led her to the edge of it and she sat down. "So are you having a good birthday so far?" he asked.

"Very good," she said. "The best."

He knelt down and kissed her gently, then wrapped his arms around her waist and kissed her harder. She lay back on the bed while he tugged at her sweater. She sighed happily. Alex's parents and brothers were away for the weekend. They were totally alone. This was the perfect chance to sleep over at Alex's and see where the whole thing would lead. But the thought of his parents made her jolt upright. "I should call my parents." They would be waiting up for her until twelve a.m., when she was due home, but she wanted to stay over with Alex. She had fantasies of waking up in the morning to orange juice and coffee, scrambling eggs with him and making toast and then kissing some more over the breakfast table and the morning paper. But for that to happen, she'd have to make sure her parents weren't expecting her home at midnight.

"What time is your curfew?" Alex asked. "I'll make sure you get home in time."

She smiled at him. He was so thoughtful and

sweet. But Haley didn't want to go home for her curfew. She didn't want to go home at all. And she thought she knew what to do.

"Just let me call them. I want to stay here tonight. All night."

"Are you sure?" Alex asked. "Won't you get caught?"

"Trust me, I know just what to say. One second." She ran downstairs to get her cell from her bag. She dialed home and told her mother she was staying over at Annie Armstrong's house for the night.

"All right, honey," Joan Miller said. "Have a good time."

Joan bought it. Awesome. Everything taken care of. Haley ran back upstairs to pick up things with Alex where they had left off.

Alex was waiting for her on the bed. "All cool?"

"All cool." She lay down beside him. They began kissing again, and soon they were tugging at each other's clothes. Alex slipped off Haley's sweater, then unfastened her skirt, while she undid the top button on his trousers and slipped her hand inside his pants. She felt the hard bulge inside his boxers as Alex gasped. He pulled down the covers and took Haley in his arms while she pulled off his pants. They were now naked except for their underwear. Haley felt warm and giddy and nervous, and as Alex pressed himself up against her, she shivered with delight.

"It's going to be amazing to sleep in your arms all night long," she whispered, hardly able to believe what they were about to do.

"It's going to be even more amazing not sleeping in your arms," Alex joked, slipping his hand down over Haley's breast, then down farther, across her stomach, and down even farther, lifting up the waistband of her ecru lace underwear.

Just then the doorbell rang. Haley glanced at the clock on the night table: it was before midnight. Had they really been fooling around for over an hour? She sat up nervously.

"Who do you think that is?" she asked.

Alex shrugged, pulling on his pants. "I don't know. Maybe one of the neighbors has an emergency."

"Haley! Are you in there?" a man's voice called from outside.

Haley froze with fear. "Oh no. That sounded like my dad."

"Your dad? But I thought you took care of that!"

"So did I." Haley jumped out of bed and peeked through the window. Sure enough, her father's hybrid SUV was in front of the house, the engine still running.

"Oh my God, it's both of my parents!" she cried. She fumbled around for her clothes. Alex buttoned up his pants and pulled on an undershirt. The doorbell rang again, this time more urgently.

"I'll go answer the door," he said. "What should I tell them?"

"Just say we were having dinner and dessert ran late," Haley said.

"Will they buy that?"

"No," Haley said. "I don't know. But we can't tell them what we were really doing!"

"No, we can't." The doorbell rang again. Alex hurried downstairs. Haley yanked on her sweater and ran after him.

Alex opened the door. There stood Perry Miller looking upset and worried, but most of all disappointed. "Haley! What's going on here?" he demanded. "Your mother said you called and told her you were staying over at Annie's, but then Blythe called about an emergency revision to a brief."

"We were just having dinner," Haley said as Perry eyed all the candles suspiciously. "I was headed over to Annie's at midnight, my new curfew, remember?"

Perry frowned. "Sure you were."

Haley caught sight of herself in the hall mirror and understood why her father was skeptical. Her hair was tousled, her cheeks were flushed and her sweater was on inside out. She looked very much like a girl who'd just been caught mid-hookup—not like someone who'd been daintily eating chocolate cake. Her parents weren't stupid.

Haley closed her eyes in defeat. She should have known better. Of course Joan Miller and Blythe Armstrong spoke often and compared notes on more than just their caseloads at work. Joan was bound to find out whether or not Haley was sleeping over at Annie's.

"Come on, Haley. We're going home." Perry led her out of the house by the arm.

"Sorry, Alex," Haley called back. "Thanks for the birthday dinner!"

She got into the backseat of the car and waved forlornly to Alex as her parents drove away. "Yes, you'd better wave goodbye," her mother said sharply. "You won't be seeing him again for a long time—if ever."

"What?"

"You heard your mother," Perry said. "You're grounded. Maybe for the rest of your life."

"Well, at least for another year, until you turn eighteen."

"What?" Haley shrieked. "You can't do that!"

But in fact, that was just what they did.

• • •

Haley should have known that her mother would check out her story with Annie's mother. After all, they work together. And as a lawyer, Joan Miller is trained not to take what people say at face value. She has learned to

dig deeper, and it didn't take much digging to figure out what Haley was up to that night. Alex was perfectly willing to take Haley home before curfew, but she let her fantasies carry her away. She won't be making that mistake again.

Hang your head and go back to page 1.

DEAD END

MAKE CURFEW

Following the rules doesn't mean you can't have fun.

Alex led Haley into the den, which was also filled with candles, and sat her down on the edge of the sofa. "Are you having a good birthday so far?" he asked.

"Very good," she said. "The best."

Alex knelt down and kissed her gently, then wrapped his arms around her waist. Haley lay back on the sofa while he snuggled up next to her tugging at her sweater. She sighed happily. Alex's parents and brothers were away for the weekend. This was the perfect chance to get to know each other better—physically. They still had an hour and a half to kill before Haley had to be home for curfew. She had fantasies of staying the whole night, waking up in the morning to orange juice and coffee, scrambling eggs with Alex, making toast and kissing some more over the breakfast table and morning paper. But Haley knew there was no way her parents would ever buy the story that she had suddenly decided to sleep over at Annie's. It was better to play it safe, and still play around a little with Alex before heading home to her own bed that night.

"What's the matter?" Alex asked.

"I wish we could spend the whole night together," Haley said.

"Me too," he said, nibbling her ear. "I'll make sure to get you home in time for curfew. We don't want you grounded so that you can't come over and do this again."

She smiled at him. "And what are we going to do?" she asked suggestively. Alex's thoughtfulness made her want to spend the night with him even more. She knew she could trust him. She rubbed her nose playfully against his cheek and snuggled up against him. "I don't want to think about going home yet. It's so cold outside and so warm in here. . . ."

"I know," he said, kissing her lightly. "But we still have a while before we have to leave. . . ."

However much time they had, it wasn't enough

for Haley. She bit Alex's lip playfully. They started making out, hot and heavy. Soon, her sweater and skirt were beside them on the floor, and Alex's pants were undone. Haley had never gone this far with a boy before, but it felt totally right. She knew she could go all the way with Alex and still feel safe, or she could stop short and do just about everything but, and that would be okay too. *So this is what it feels like to be in a real relationship,* she thought. *I could get used to this.*

They continued hooking up, exploring each other's bodies until well after eleven p.m. Alex lay beside her, holding her and touching her hair. He lifted his head and glanced at the clock. "It's almost midnight. Better get you home before you turn into a pumpkin."

They kissed once more, then got off the sofa and put on their clothes. Alex went outside a few minutes early to warm up the car. "Brrr!" he said when he came back in. Haley was warming her hands on a mug of tea, which she shared with him. "It's freezing out there!" He made sure she was all bundled up before they went out to face the cold.

Haley hurried out to the car, her breath clouding the air. Inside it was toasty warm. Alex got in and drove her home. The streets were quiet and still.

He pulled up in front of her house, keeping the car running for warmth. "We still have five minutes," Haley said.

"Let's not waste them." Alex leaned toward her and they kissed until the last possible second. When the clock struck midnight, Haley gave him one last peck. "Good night," she said, slipping out of the car and running into the house. She peered out the front window and flicked the porch light off and on as a wink goodbye. Alex flashed his headlights and drove away into the darkness.

Haley floated up to her bedroom, feeling happy and right and totally in love. Everything with Alex was turning out to be just perfect, and that was all right with her.

THE END

DATE WITH DWI

Strange boys + strange cars + drinking = big trouble.

Haley looked at Rob, the cutie with the glasses, behind the wheel of his sports car. He seemed like a nice enough guy. And a party at an estate sounded like fun.

It's your birthday, she told herself. *Live a little.* Besides, the party was only a few blocks away. What was the worst that could happen?

She got into the car. Rob revved the engine and sped away from the curb. Haley grabbed on to the dashboard to steady herself.

"Slow down," she said. "There's no rush."

"I always drive like this," Rob said. "It's okay. Besides, what's the point of having a sports car if you don't go fast?"

In the close confines of the car Haley could smell the liquor on his breath. "How much have you had to drink tonight?" she asked.

"Just that stuff Matt brought to the dance," Rob said. "Chillax."

They roared up the street, but before they'd driven two blocks Haley saw flashing lights and heard a siren behind them. She looked back. A police car was tailing them, red lights glaring. "Pull over!" the officer shouted over the loudspeaker.

Rob groaned. "Oh no, not again."

"Not again?" Haley said. "This has happened before?"

"Every time I drink and drive I get pulled over. It's so unfair."

He stopped the car. A police officer approached the driver's side and knocked on the window. Rob rolled it down.

"License and registration, please," the officer said. She leaned into the car and got a whiff of Rob's breath. "Whew!" She waved her hand in front of her nose. "Son, I'm going to need you to get out of the car."

While the first police officer gave Rob a sobriety

test—which he promptly failed—her partner opened Haley's door and asked her to get out too.

"Where were you tonight?" the policeman asked her.

"At a school dance," Haley said. "I haven't done anything wrong."

"Can I see some ID?"

Haley showed him her brand-new license.

"This one's been drinking," the policewoman said, jerking her thumb at Rob. "We'd better take them both to the station."

The police officers led Haley and Rob to the squad car and locked them into the backseat. Rob was on the verge of tears.

"I can't get arrested!" he said. "My parents are going to kill me! Or at least take my car away."

"Maybe they should," Haley said.

"No! I'm nothing without that car!"

What a jerk, Haley thought, but then she thought about her own parents. They wouldn't be too happy about this little turn of events either.

At the police station, Rob was charged with a DWI and led away to a holding cell. "Sorry, son," the officer said. "You're going to night court."

Haley sat in a waiting room while the other officer called her parents. They arrived minutes later with Mitchell in tow.

"Thank you for calling us, officer," Perry Miller said. "We'll take her home now."

Joan Miller took Haley by the arm and practically dragged her out to the car. "What on earth were you thinking? Underage drinking? Driving with a drunk boy you barely know? Who was he, anyway?"

Haley had to struggle to remember his name. "I think his name was Rob."

"You think?" Haley's mother was livid. "You get into a car with a boy who's been drinking and you don't even know his name? Young lady, you are lucky to be alive."

"Too bad you'll have to spend the rest of your life in your room," Perry said.

"What? That's a prison sentence!" Haley protested.

"It's better than going to jail for real," her mother said. "I think."

"That's right," her father said. "Haley Miller, you are grounded for life."

"Ha-ha," Mitchell singsonged. "Haley's grounded forever. Haley's grounded forever."

"Or at least a full year, until you turn eighteen," Joan added.

• • •

One small slip of judgment and Haley's life is ruined. Of course, it could have been a lot worse—Rob, or whatever his name is, could have crashed the car and maimed or even killed Haley, in which case she would have wished she were only grounded for life. There's

nothing wrong with a little adventure, but you should at least know whose car you're getting into before you zoom off into the sunset.

Hang your head and go back to page 1.

DEAD END

HOME GAME

All's fair in love and basketball.

"Whoo! Go Ridgewood!"

Coco cheered as she and her friends filed into the bleachers on the visitors' side. Haley felt weird sitting across the gym among strange Ridgewood students, most of whom she didn't even know, to cheer on her school's rival team.

But that was the idea. Coco's idea, anyway: to really make the Hillsdale bad boys feel it—to show Reese, Spencer, Drew and Johnny how much their ex-girlfriends did not need them, to show how far the girls had left them behind. The Coquettes were hanging with a new crowd now, Matt Graham's Ridgewood crowd—that was the message Coco wanted to send. Haley saw the logic in it but it still felt wrong cheering against their own school.

The game began and Ridgewood started out strong. Matt scored three points in the first few minutes against a flailing Hillsdale defense. At the end of the first quarter Ridgewood was up by four.

"Yes! Ridgewood rocks!" Coco cheered. Haley, Cecily, Whitney and Sasha joined in, yelling for their new favorite Bergen County team.

"Hillsdale boys are totally lame!" Sasha shouted.

"Go back to fondling bikini babes!" Cecily called. That got a few laughs.

Haley saw Reese look up at them from center court with a determined gleam in his eye. *Uh-oh*. Haley knew that look. He was fired up.

He went into a huddle with Spencer, Johnny and Drew. "What are you doing, planning your next beach vacation?" Coco taunted. "Be sure to bring lots of those cute little umbrellas for your drinks!"

The Hillsdale boys jogged onto the court to start the second quarter. Right away they looked like a different team. Johnny stole the ball from a Ridgewood forward and dribbled down the court for two points. A few minutes later Drew intercepted a

Ridgewood pass and threw an assist to Reese, who launched one for three points. Hillsdale pulled ahead by one.

"That was a lucky shot!" Whitney yelled. "Ridgewood rules! Hillsdale boys are tools!"

The Hillsdale guys glared at them in the opposing team's stands one last time. After that they didn't look at the girls again. But the taunting had done its job. They were fired up, and soon they were playing the best basketball of their lives.

Spencer the ball-hog actually passed to Johnny, who made a beautiful layup for two more points. Reese hit every free throw he was handed—and Ridgewood was so frustrated they were fouling him all over the place. Drew was on fire, speeding down the court and mowing down Ridgewood guards like a freight train. By halftime Hillsdale had taken a commanding ten-point lead, with more to come.

Coco's crew had stopped their taunting. The whole Ridgewood side of the gym grew silent. The Hillsdale Avengers watched their exes in stunned amazement—part admiration, part fury.

"How dare they?" Coco muttered. "How dare they play so well? Last time I saw them play they looked like clumsy toddlers out there! All of a sudden they're practically pros!"

Reese launched another three-point swisher, and Haley had to stop herself from clapping and shouting,

"Yay Reese!" But not before Coco caught the telltale twitch in Haley's hands.

"What are you doing?" Coco said. "Don't cheer for them! Traitor."

"You have to admit they're looking awesome out there, Coco," Sasha said. "Even Spencer's playing well."

"Even Spencer's playing well," Coco echoed in a mocking tone. Spencer was well known as the weak link on the team, and Haley knew Coco didn't appreciate having that fact thrown in her face, even if they were cheering against the boys.

Coco grumbled as Drew hit another layup, but by the fourth quarter the girls had been stunned into awed silence. Haley found herself containing her excitement as she watched Reese glide down the court and soar into the air. He was really good when he was on, she had to admit it. He was a star.

The game ended on a last-second rebound by Johnny, who dunked the ball as the buzzer sounded. Hillsdale whipped Ridgewood this time, 68–56. The Hillsdale portion of the crowd erupted into cheers of joy, waving signs and tossing confetti onto the victorious players, while Haley and her friends sat, lonely and quiet, on the wrong side of the gym. Even Coco got caught up in the celebration, trying to catch Spencer's eye as the boys jogged off the court. But he wouldn't look at her, and Haley couldn't get Reese's attention, either. None of the boys even glanced their way.

"They're ignoring us," Cecily said.

"Jerks," Coco said. "Just because they finally won a game they think they're the hottest thing since jalapeños."

"Well, we are sitting with the opposing team," Haley reminded them. "It's kind of a big insult. I mean, I can see how the boys would see it that way."

"It was supposed to be an insult," Coco snapped. "It was supposed to insult them and destroy their confidence so they would lose the game. They were supposed to be on their knees groveling before us by now—not ignoring us."

"That was the plan," Sasha said. "But it backfired."

"We don't need them," Coco said. "They're just ridiculous high school boys anyway. We're too good for these children. What we need are college boys. Real, sexy, mature, adoring college boys."

"Sounds fabulous," Whitney said. "But where are we going to find some?"

"At the college boy store," Coco said.

"The what?" Whitney asked.

"The most famous purveyor of college boys in the country," Coco said. "The top luxury brand. Yale."

"Mmm, Yale boys," Cecily said. "Yum."

"Spring break is just around the corner, so I propose a road trip. A little visit to my big sister, Ali. I'm sure she'll love the company."

Coco's sister, Ali, was a freshman at Yale and already hobnobbing with the jet-set crowd. If anyone could provide hot boys, it was Ali. And luckily, Yale's spring break came two weeks before Hillsdale's, so the boys would all be tan and the campus would be buzzing.

"Sounds perfect," Haley said. "We'll go in your car, right, Coco?" It seemed logical: Coco had been given a sizeable luxury sedan for her birthday, and it was by far the roomiest and most comfortable car any of the girls had.

"Can't," Coco said. "It's going back to the dealer for an upgrade that week. I won't get the new car until after our spring break."

"Okay, so there's always Stallion," Haley said, glancing at Sasha, whose vintage Mustang wasn't exactly plush but at least had style going for it.

Sasha shook her head. "Stallion's going into the shop again for repairs. I love him but reliable he isn't. We'd be lucky just to make it to New Haven."

"What about you, Haley?" Coco turned her steely blue eyes on her. "Didn't you get a car for your birthday?"

Haley'd been dreading this moment. Yes, she had gotten a car for her birthday. And no, she never wanted to be seen in public behind the wheel. She knew Coco wouldn't tolerate it either. Nor would anyone else at school. Haley would be teased unmercifully.

In fact, it was for this very reason that Haley had

yet to drive Gam Polly's ancient sedan. The corny bumper stickers alone made her nauseated. Haley had tried everything, but they wouldn't come off. Perhaps some future generation would find these bumper stickers charming, but Haley found them absolutely cringeworthy.

But the worst thing about the car was the violent way it backfired. It sounded like Texas on the first day of hunting season and sent anyone within earshot running for cover. It was as if the car wanted to draw extra attention to its ugly self.

"Why don't we take the train?" Haley suggested. "We can go into the city, grab some coffee in Grand Central . . . it'll be romantic."

"No," Coco said firmly. "We need wheels. Haley, I could swear I heard you mention getting a car at some point."

"Well, I do kind of sort of have a car," Haley said. "But you're not going to like it."

"How bad could it be? A car's a car," Cecily said.

"What is it, like maroon or something?" Whitney asked. Of course that was the worst possible thing she could imagine.

But Haley knew better. There were far worse things a car could be beyond maroon.

● ● ●

Haley's going to have to bust out her grandma car sometime. And meeting some college boys might be the fresh

start she needs on the romantic front. If you think she should go through with this road trip and drive the girls to Yale, turn to page 288, SPRING BREAK AT YALE.

Alternately, if you think the girls should stay home and try to repair what's left of their relationships with their old boyfriends, go to page 301, REESE ON HIS KNEES.

DARK VICTORY

Nobody loves a doormat.

"Haley, please! Don't leave me here alone. Do you really have to go to class right now?"

Haley stared at the new Devon, slumped against his locker with a bouquet of flowers—the fourth one that week—crushed against his leather jacket. He hadn't changed his style—his hair and his clothes were the same—but somehow, to Haley, he just didn't look cool anymore. Maybe it was the way he followed her everywhere like a whipped puppy, whining for her attention.

"Sorry, Devon, but I've got a Spanish test," she lied. She actually didn't even have class then. She just needed to get away from her new shadow for a while.

"Good luck on the test! I'll wait for you here!"

She couldn't even bear to turn around and wave to him as she walked away. She knew what she'd see if she did: Devon with his adorable mop of hair and big sad eyes pleading *Love me love me love me, but don't ever leave.*

She had thought she did love him, once. And for a while she was thrilled with all the attention. But Irene's plan had worked a little too well, and now she saw Devon in a completely different light. An unflattering light that showed every crack and fault in his personality.

Once he'd been cool. Now he was just a pathetic, lovesick dog.

She went back to her locker three hours later, figuring the coast had to be clear by then. But he was still there waiting for her, the sad flowers wilted and dying, petals littering the floor. He brightened at the sight of her.

"You're back! Look—I bought you a chocolate bar. You like chocolate, right? Everybody likes chocolate."

Who was this lovebot? She hardly even recognized him anymore.

She took the chocolate bar and opened it. At

this point she needed something to give her extra energy—carrying the weight of Devon's devotion was hard work. Or it felt like work, anyway. Was that how love was supposed to feel? Haley didn't think so.

"Do you need anything?" Devon asked. "More flowers, maybe?"

"Enough with the flowers," Haley snapped. "I never thought I could get so sick of flowers."

"They are sickening. You're right." Devon sneered at the flowers he was holding and tossed them into a nearby trash can. "What was I thinking?"

Haley opened her locker to get her things and go home for the day. Devon crept up behind her and started rubbing her shoulders. "How was the Spanish test? I bet you aced it."

She shrugged him off. "Get your hands off me. I didn't ask for a back rub."

"Sorry. Sorry sorry." He shrank back like a chastened puppy—which was even more infuriating.

"What are you doing tonight?" Devon asked. "Want to see a movie?"

"I can't," Haley said. "I'm busy."

"What about tomorrow night?"

"I'm busy tomorrow night too. I'm busy for the rest of my life."

He laughed in a panicky way. "You're so funny! That's hilarious."

Haley rolled her eyes. "Yeah. Hilarious. See you."

"Sure you don't want a ride?"

"Positive."

"Okay. I'll call you in an hour to make sure you got home okay."

"Don't bother."

"It's no bother!"

Ugh. Haley went straight to Drip to meet Irene for a powwow. School wasn't safe—Devon might find them there.

"We've created a monster," Haley said. "Your plan was brilliant. I'm just starting to wish I hadn't gotten what I asked for. Devon used to be so cool! Now he's unbearable."

"I couldn't agree more," Irene said. "It's disgusting the way he follows you around, begging you to give him an order. I miss the old Devon. I'm worried about him, actually."

"I wish the old Devon would come back too," Haley said. "I liked our friendship a lot better before it was all about me. I can't take the pressure! Irene, what should I do?"

"The answer is obvious, dummy," Irene said. "Just start being nice to him again. Quit playing ice queen and give a little to the relationship. You literally have to kill his puppy love with kindness. Maybe that will even things out a bit."

"I don't know if I want to," Haley said. "I can hardly look at the guy."

"You have to," Irene warned. "If you care about

his feelings at all, even as a friend, you've got to stop ignoring him and start being nice again. Unless you hate to give up the one man fan club."

"I'm sick of the fan club," Haley said. "The fan club is stalking me!"

"Haley, I'm serious," Irene said. "Don't take this game too far or you'll ruin your friendship with Devon. And then I'll be mad. And Shaun will be pissed that you hurt his friend's feelings. And you might find yourself without any friends at all. Any interesting friends, anyway."

Haley absorbed Irene's words. *She's been right about everything so far,* Haley thought. *Maybe I should listen to her.*

• • •

If you think Haley should start being nicer to Devon and try to restore their friendship, turn to page 285, EQUILIBRIUM RESTORED. If you think Haley should tell Devon how she feels and cut him loose, turn to page 279, SLOPPY SECONDS. Finally, if you think Haley should forget about Devon and go find some new boys to kick around, turn to page 288, SPRING BREAK AT YALE.

SLOPPY SECONDS

Honesty is rarely the best policy when it's heartless.

"Hey, Haley." There he was, the now ever-present Devon, waiting for her at her locker first thing in the morning as he had been every morning for the past two weeks. "Look what I made for you."

She could hardly bear to look at another trinket Devon had crafted for her by hand, but morbid curiosity made her turn and see. He'd silk-screened a T-shirt with a picture of her face, large and iconic as a Warhol image. On the back it said, in sparkling gold letters, "My Goddess."

Haley shook her head wearily. She wanted to disappear into her locker and stay there for the rest of her life. "You're going to wear that around all day?" she asked.

"All day, every day. I've made a Haley shirt for every day of the week. Kind of like day-of-the-week underwear. Don't some girls have those?"

"No, no, no," Haley muttered. "At least put a jacket over it. It's hideous!"

"Whatever you say, She Who Makes the Sun Rise." He shrugged into his jacket. "You're right as always, gorgeous. It looks much better with a jacket. Hey, maybe I could silk-screen your image on a jean jacket. . . ."

That was it. Haley couldn't take it anymore. Irene had told her to go easy on Devon, to try tempering his adoration gently, with a little sympathy. But she just didn't have it in her anymore. He'd worn all her sympathy away.

There was only one thing left to try: brutal honesty.

"Devon, listen," she began. "We've got to talk."

He straightened up eagerly. If he'd had a tail, it would have been wagging.

"I know you like me—"

"I more than like you, Haley. You know that."

"Right. I know you worship me and all, but I'm beginning to think I might not be the right girl for you."

His face fell. In her mind she could see the tail drooping. "Don't say that, gorgeous. You know I can't live without you."

"You lived without me before, Devon," Haley said. "You can do it again. You'll be fine."

The color began to drain from his cheeks as it dawned on him what was happening. "No . . ."

"Remember how you used to spend so much time with Darcy?" Haley said. "Not so long ago, the two of you were inseparable."

"Sure, but that was before I realized that I was born to love you forever," Devon said, a note of nervousness creeping into his voice.

"Come on, Devon. We both know that forever is a long, long time. Love should be fun. It shouldn't be a life sentence."

"A life sentence?" Devon's hands were shaking now. "Is that how you think of us? As a kind of prison?"

Kind of, Haley thought, but she wasn't brutally honest enough to say that out loud. "I'm just saying that I think maybe Darcy is better suited for you. She's a lot punkier than I am, really. My punk thing is just a pose. Don't tell anyone, but it's true. I'm really straitlaced at heart."

"I don't believe you," Devon said. "There's nothing phony about you. You could never fake the creative individual you are."

Haley flinched. She hated that lovey-dovey talk.

That wasn't the Devon she'd once crushed on so fiercely. "See, I hate to hear you talk that way, Devon. It's not the real you. You're like a zombie or something now."

"This is absolutely the real me. The me I discovered through you! Haley, don't let the real me die. Don't kill him! Don't break his heart! I beg you!"

Haley shook her head. "Now I don't even understand what you're talking about. Look, I'm trying to help you out here. Give Darcy a call, see what she's up to. You'll feel a lot better."

She saw the whole thing play out on his face: his love and fear and pain hardening into fury. And then he let her have it.

"I get it now," he said angrily. "I see what you've been doing. You've been toying with me, haven't you? Just for fun. This was never about me, was it? It was all about you and Darcy. You played games with my heart just to show Darcy that you're the all-powerful queen, ruler of the school, that she's no threat to you. You wanted to prove to her that if you wanted me you could have me, no matter how much she might have wanted me too. That's what was going on, wasn't it?"

Haley didn't know what to say. She was shocked at his sudden change of mood, at how quickly he could turn on her. But she also had to admit there was a kernel of truth in what he'd said. She'd liked Devon for a long time, but she never really made an effort with him until Darcy staked her claim. Then, suddenly, Haley had to have him.

But that was all in the past. Now that she had him, she saw that she didn't really want him. What could she do about it now? Pretend to like him more than she did? It was impossible.

Her silence seemed to confirm his worst suspicions. "I was right from the start. I knew it." He took off his jacket and tore the Haley T-shirt off in disgust. "You know what, Haley? You're a Cocobot at heart."

"What? I am not," Haley protested.

"You are. I don't know why you bother spending time with freaks like me and Shaun and Irene. You belong with Coco and her crowd—superficial tarts who use other people to get what they want. From now on, hang with them. They're your real people. And stay away from me and Shaun and Irene—and Darcy, too. Because you know what? I'm going to take your advice, Haley, and give Darcy a call. I'm going to see if she'll forgive me for treating her as shabbily as you've treated me."

He stepped on the T-shirt, grinding his boot into the silk-screened image of her face. Then he walked away, leaving Haley struggling to get her bearings. She couldn't deny it; she knew he was right. She'd been mean and manipulative. And she couldn't just blame Irene. Haley deserved every word Devon spat at her and more.

• • •

Haley's big mistake: letting her power over Devon go to her head, and thinking he was too drunk with love to understand what was going on. He really told her off, though. Let's hope she's learned her lesson and won't lead a boy around on a leash like that again.

If only she'd shown him a little more kindness, a little compassion, she might have been able to salvage their friendship. Now Haley has lost not only that friendship but also the goodwill of the whole art crew. She may have no choice but to become a Cocobot, if she wants to have any friends—but it's unlikely Coco will have her. Coco doesn't take the art crowd's rejects. And remember, Haley still has that green streak in her hair.

Hang your head and go back to page 1.

DEAD END

EQUILIBRIUM RESTORED

The difference between brutal honesty and compassionate honesty can mean the difference between anger and friendship.

Devon showed up at school the next day wearing Haley's worst nightmare: a T-shirt with her face silk-screened on the front and the words "My Goddess" in gold on the back. That was the last straw. She could hardly stand the sight of him at the moment, but deep down she didn't want to ruin their friendship. He was a good guy, she knew that. She also knew that nothing turned him off like niceness.

"What do you think?" he asked, showing off the new T-shirt. "I made it myself."

"It's great, Devon!" Haley lied. "You're so good at silk-screening."

"Thanks." Devon looked pleased.

"I wish I were as artistic as you are," Haley said. "I really admire that in people."

"Thanks." At the second compliment in a row, the glow in his face faded ever so slightly. *Keep going,* Haley told herself. *You're making progress.*

She stepped closer and touched his arm. "Maybe we should go to a museum or something this weekend. Together. Afterward we can go out for a romantic dinner. What do you think?"

"Uh, sure. That sounds great, Haley." He moved his arm away from her caressing fingers. She took his hand instead. He tried to tug it away, but she held it firmly.

"I'm so glad we're finally getting so much closer," she said. "I've waited for this moment for so long."

"You have?" Devon said. "That's funny. A few minutes ago you seemed like you didn't really care about me."

"I care," Haley said. "You know I do."

Now he looked scared. "This is kind of sudden. . . ."

"Say it," Haley said. "Call me your goddess."

"My what?"

"You know. Like it says on the shirt."

"Oh right. The shirt." He looked down at the Haley T-shirt as if he was reconsidering it now, and shrugged into his jacket. It covered the shirt nicely. "This was really just a joke, kind of."

Haley laughed. She'd broken the spell; that was clear. Enough sweet talk. Now it was time to come clean.

"What are you laughing about?" he asked. "You sure are acting weird this morning."

"I'm sorry, Devon," Haley said. "I was teasing you a little bit before. It's just that I started feeling like things were getting kind of out of hand between us. Too intense. You know what I mean?"

He nodded and looked relieved. "You're right. It's my fault. I went way overboard."

"It's all right," Haley said. "It's just . . . I missed being friends with you. I liked things the way they were. Do you think we can go back to hanging with Irene and Shaun and keeping things cool between us for a while, before we start proposing to each other?"

"Yeah, totally," Devon said. "I'd like that too."

He slinked away down the hall. The old, cool Devon was back. Haley just hoped this wouldn't mean the resurgence of the old, cruel Darcy. But that was the risk she had to take. If she and Devon were going to be friends, she'd have to deal with that possibility too.

THE END

SPRING BREAK AT YALE

Just being on an Ivy League campus doesn't make you smart.

"I don't believe this," Coco muttered. "Why didn't you warn me?"

"I did warn you," Haley said. "You didn't listen."

Haley's pale yellow grandma-mobile backfired for the umpteenth time just as they pulled up in front of Ali's dorm at Yale. Three cute Elis turned their heads, startled at the noise, and sneered at the hideous car.

"I can't believe I'm driving up to Yale in this car

from hell," Coco groaned. "Hide me please, Sasha. I think I'll just curl up and die right now."

In her rearview mirror Haley saw Coco slump down in the backseat, hoping no one would see her arriving in the least stylish way possible. She tried not to take it personally.

"I'm sorry, my parents don't believe in wasting money on a new car when this one still works," Haley said. "If you didn't have to upgrade your perfectly good car every six months we wouldn't be in this mess."

"Go ahead, blame it on me," Coco sniffed. "But if my grandmother even looked at a car this ugly I'd have her removed from the family tree. This is a nightmare."

Cecily tried to cheer them up. "It's not a big deal, Coco. We'll park the car and walk everywhere from now on. No one has to know our tight little butts ever touched these Naugahyde seats."

"No one except the hundreds of people who already saw us driving up in this boat," Coco said.

"Um, she has a name, it's the Lemon," Haley said, trying to make light of their situation.

"This has to be the most embarrassing moment of my entire life," Coco said, and Haley could feel the team turning on her.

Haley parked the car and sighed. She was embarrassed too. She hated Gam Polly's car and wished

Coco hadn't forced her to drive them to New Haven. But now that it was done she also wished Coco would stop whining about it.

"Everything will be fine once we change into our hottest threads and show these Yale boys what they've been missing," Whitney said.

The girls piled out of the car. Haley opened the trunk to get their bags.

"Hide me, Haley." Coco insisted on cowering behind Haley's coat so that no one would know she'd just stepped out of the old-lady shuttle.

They lugged their bags up two flights to Ali's suite in Davenport College. Luckily Ali's roommates were away for the weekend, so there was plenty of room for Coco and friends to take over. Not that Ali looked pleased about it.

"Coco, I told you you could bring one friend, not four," Ali complained. "How is it going to look, me being trailed everywhere by five high school kids?"

"It's going to look fabulous, because we're going to look fabulous," Coco said. "I call this bed." She set her bag down on the best bed in the one empty room in the suite. "Two of you are going to have to sleep on the couch."

Cecily took the other bed in Coco's room, and Sasha took the empty bed in Ali's room, which left Haley to share the pullout couch in the common room with Whitney.

"What's on for tonight?" Coco asked Ali.

"Cocktail party? Dinner at a nice restaurant? Maybe a frat blowout?"

"There's a party at Zeta Psi," Ali said with a yawn. "I suppose it wouldn't be too mortifying to be seen with you there. You could blend in with the clueless second-semester transfers."

"Thanks for the warm welcome, Ali," Coco said sarcastically. "It means a lot to us."

"Hey—you invited yourselves up here," Ali said. "It's not my responsibility to make sure you have a good time. I'm a busy college student. I've got fashion magazines to read."

She buried herself in the latest glossy while her little sister and friends threw open their bags and started pulling out clothes.

"Let's get dressed for the party," Coco said. She held up two dresses: one a simple blue sheath, the other a micro-mini baby-doll number. "Which dress screams college sophisticate? And don't be wrong."

"Oooh, the baby-doll!" Whitney said.

"I like the sheath," Cecily said. "But only if you dress it up with jewelry—maybe an armload of bangle bracelets?" She unzipped her jewelry case and jangled a stack of metal bangles.

Ali sighed and slammed her magazine shut. "You know what? I think I'll do my reading in a café somewhere. Have fun without me."

"Aren't you going to get dressed for the party?" Haley asked.

"Uh, hello?" Ali said. "It's just a stupid frat party. I don't need three hours to get ready for that."

"Don't listen to her," Coco said. "She's trying to make the party sound lame so we won't stay in her stupid dump of a suite longer than necessary. Now, on to hair accessories . . ."

The girls spent hours dolling themselves up to their idea of the height of sophistication with clothes, hair and makeup. Just before they left the suite to grab some dinner, Haley caught sight of herself in the mirror and paused. She'd never worn so much makeup before.

"Are you sure all this eyeliner looks okay?" she asked the room in general.

"It looks amazing," Coco said. "Stop worrying. It looks like a lot in this harsh dorm light, but at a nighttime party your eyes will seem smoky and mysterious."

"All right," Haley agreed, and out they went into the New Haven evening.

First stop, Mory's, the venerable Yale club. They walked in but a bouncer stopped them just inside the door. "Can I see your student IDs, ladies?"

"We left them in our dorm," Coco lied as she tried to breeze past him. He blocked her with a beefy arm.

"Sorry, Mory's is for Yale students, alumni or faculty only," he said. "And besides, if you girls are thinking about going to the bar, I'd forget it. You're obviously way too young to drink."

Coco tried to finesse this by laughing coyly. "Aren't you sweet. Did you hear that, girls? This adorable young man actually thinks we're teenagers!"

The bouncer rolled his eyes. "You are teenagers. See you in a few years." He gently pushed them toward the door. They found themselves out on the cold, hard street, unsure of where to go next.

"We're not meeting Ali at Zeta Psi until nine," Coco said.

"And I'm starving," Whitney said.

"What about Pepe's Pizza?" Sasha said, nodding at a pizza joint down the block. "New Haven is supposed to have the best pies on the planet."

The line at Pepe's was out the door, but the girls had time to kill, so they waited. Whitney complained about hunger pangs the entire time. At last they got a table and sat down to share a large mushroom pie.

"This is such a waste! After all our hard work dieting, we're ingesting empty pizza calories?" Coco said, half disgusted, though not so much that she couldn't devour a yummy slice.

"Who cares? It's delicious," Haley said.

At nine o'clock they trooped across campus to the frat party. They passed roving gangs of students laughing, partying, having fun. They also passed the library, where, through the windows, they could see other students hard at work.

"Look at those grinds," Coco said. "Don't they

know that the whole point of college is partying? They're missing all the fun!"

By the time they found Zeta Psi the party was in full swing, but there was no sign of Ali. "Who cares?" Coco said. "We don't need her. Now point me to the college boys."

The house was old and worn—Haley could see the remnants of parties gone by on the scuffed walls and scratched furniture. Most of the partygoers were gathered around a bar in the basement that smelled of stale beer. "You can definitely tell boys live here," Haley said.

The crowd was fairly preppy, with boys in jeans and button-downs and sweaters and girls in jeans or leggings and sexy tops and sweaters. Very few girls wore dresses, and Haley began to understand what Ali meant when she'd said it was "just a stupid frat party." In her silver miniskirt and heavy eyeliner, Haley suddenly felt as if she'd dressed for a costume ball.

A guy with a long neck poking through his argyle sweater took one look at the girls and broke into a big grin. "Hey look, the jailbait's arrived," he announced. A few of the Yale girls glanced over at the Coco crowd and rolled their eyes. To Haley's dismay, Coco didn't seem to pick up on the signals: everyone at the party saw through them immediately. They were obviously still just high school girls.

"Those old hags are just jealous of us," Coco said.

"Let's go steal some boys from under their wrinkled noses."

"They're only a couple of years older than we are," Sasha protested as Coco sashayed into the fray. Trailed by her posse, she bypassed the boy who had called her jailbait and infiltrated a group of intellectual types by the bar.

"As I see it, Gide is a direct descendant of Dostoyevsky," a guy with a shaved head said. "Except instead of condemning the morality of Nietzsche's so-called superman, he is actually making a case for moral emptiness."

"You've got it all wrong," a guy who was chewing on an unlit pipe said. "Sure, Gide makes a case for gratuitous murder, but then he dismantles it."

Coco tried to interject. "Gide is French, right? See these shoes?" She held out her delicate foot shod in an expensive designer shoe. "They're French too. I got them on my last trip to Paris."

The bald guy stared at her in disbelief. "You're not in my Modern Literature class, are you?"

"Modern literature?" Coco said. "No. I'm taking old-fashioned literature."

The guys laughed. "She's joking, right?" the pipe-chewer said.

Coco laughed along with them. "Will you get me a drink, please? I'd love some champagne."

"Sorry, we only have beer and . . . beer," the bald guy said.

"Okay, beer, then," Coco said.

The pipe-chewer laughed. "How old are you—twelve?"

"All these girls look like kids to me," a guy with short dreadlocks said.

"We're not twelve," Whitney said. "We're freshmen. We just look dewier and more bright-eyed than usual."

"But we're very experienced," Coco said suggestively.

The guys burst out laughing again. "How many times have you heard that?" the bald guy said. "Come on, tell the truth: you go to Notre Dame High, right? Or is it St. Francis?"

"Don't let them have anything to drink," the pipe-chewer said. "We could get arrested just for talking to them."

Three beefy lacrosse types intervened. "What have we here?" said a guy with a blond buzz cut. "Hello, girls. Why are you wasting your time talking to these eggheads when you could be making out with us?"

"Yeah," said a thick-necked guy with an earring. "Can we give you girls a tour of the house? Have you seen the weight room?"

"The weight room?" Whitney said. "No, we haven't seen anything like that yet. Come on! Let's go on a tour!"

"Let's get these girls some beers," the third lacrosse player said.

"Finally," Coco said. "Let's ditch the nerds, girls."

They started to follow the jocks upstairs. Haley had a bad feeling about this, but Coco was obviously so humiliated by the intellectual guys that she was looking for a way to salvage the night—even if it meant hanging with these beefy boys who were not her type and clearly trouble.

"Wait a second," she said to Coco, trying to stall. "Shouldn't we look around for Ali?"

"I'm right here." Haley turned to find Ali just walking into the party. She surveyed the situation her little sister had gotten herself into and shook her head. "Uh-uh. Tyler, just exactly what do you think you're doing with my little sister and her moronic friends?"

"This is your sister? I didn't know that, Ali," the blond buzz cut named Tyler said.

"She's my sister and she's only seventeen," Ali said. "She's off-limits, guys. They all are."

"Seventeen? Gosh, I figured she had to be at least eighteen," Tyler said insincerely.

"We were just giving them a tour," the thick-necked guy said.

"Yeah—a tour of your bedrooms," Ali said. "Come on, Coco. Let's get you girls out of here before you do something you—and I—will regret."

"Ali, you're ruining our big college night!" Coco said.

"Aw, look, I think she's going to cry," Tyler said, mocking Coco.

"Coco, you idiot, I'm saving you from the worst night of your life," Ali snapped. "Trust me. These guys are a semester away from being arrested for date rape."

The girls went back to Ali's dorm and spent the rest of the evening playing Scrabble, except for Coco, who refused to play and sulked in her room the whole time.

"This is all your fault," she kept saying to Haley. "That grandma-mobile gave our whole trip bad vibes." Haley watched as the other girls nodded in agreement. It wasn't fair. How was she entirely to blame?

The next morning, after a cafeteria breakfast, they piled into the Gam Polly sedan and drove back home to Hillsdale. "It doesn't matter that nothing actually happened last night," Coco said. She sat in the front seat, next to Haley. "The important thing is that we went to Yale. We can tell the kids at school whatever we want. The key is to make Spencer squirm with jealousy, and to keep our stories straight. So, if anyone asks, we went to a little cocktail party at somebody's fabulous off-campus apartment. Let's say the party was thrown by a British heiress, and I totally hooked up with an earl whose name was . . ."

"Earl?" Whitney suggested.

"That's too lame to even shoot down," Coco said. "No, his name is Jeremy and he's gorgeous and rich and crazy about me. . . ."

As Coco yammered on, spinning an elaborate fantasy weekend out of their disastrous night at Yale, Haley thought about Hillsdale and what awaited her there. She felt a sudden, nostalgic pang of desire for Reese Highland. There was nothing so special about those college boys, she realized. They were just like the boys she knew, only a few years older. The only boy who seemed special to her then, who seemed truly different from the average slobbering, hormone-crazed Y chromosome, was Reese. Why had she worked so hard to push him away? Lately, there had been talk around school that Reese hadn't even done anything in Nevis. And yet Haley had never given him the chance to explain. Was there any way to salvage what they'd once had? Was there any way to undo the damage and bring him back?

"No matter what happens when we get home," Coco was saying, "we've got to keep freezing the boys out. After what they did to us, they deserve to suffer as much as possible. We've got to keep twisting the knife."

"Right," Cecily, Sasha and Whitney agreed.

"Right," Haley echoed. But was it?

• • •

The Yale trip was a bust. Coco's obviously disappointed she doesn't have a college hookup story to go home with, but that won't stop her from making one up—one so good the truth could never equal it. But lying about her conquests is not Haley's style.

She faces a choice about Reese. Should she stick with Coco and her friends and stand her ground? Should she keep freezing him out even though her feelings have thawed? If you think it's the principle that counts here and Reese deserves more punishment, turn to page 310, LONELY ONE.

Or maybe you think that by now Haley is tired of listening to Coco's crackpot theories. Maybe she's sick of playing by Coco's rules and wants to follow her own heart for a change. If you think she should get her PRIORITIES STRAIGHT, turn to page 306.

There's a time for sisterhood and a time for romance. The hard part is getting the timing right.

REESE ON HIS KNEES

It's hard to follow a leader whose motto is "Do as I say, not as I do."

"Hey, Sasha." Haley was surprised to see Sasha walking arm in arm through the courtyard with her ex-boyfriend, Johnny Lane. Since they had emphatically broken up only weeks before over the Caribbean bikini-girl photos, Sasha had been one of the most hard-core supporters of Coco's Operation Dump 'Em campaign. But there she was, glowing with happiness, Johnny nuzzling her neck just like old times.

"Hey, Haley." Sasha didn't quite look her in the

eye. Feeling guilty perhaps, Haley speculated. What would Coco say when she heard that Sasha and Johnny had gotten back together? She'd completely flip, that's what Haley thought.

Later that afternoon, Haley spotted Cecily coming out of the gym with Drew. *That's weird,* Haley thought. *Cecily must have decided he needs another lecture on how much she hates him.*

But it sure didn't look as if she hated him. Drew put his arm around Cecily and gave her a kiss on the cheek. And Cecily didn't push him away; far from it. In fact, she kissed him back.

What's going on? Haley wondered. *Did I miss something*?

Last Haley had heard, Coco was insisting that they keep freezing out their cheating ex-boyfriends. So why did Cecily and Sasha suddenly seem back in boyfriend bliss?

Then, passing through the parking lot on her way home, Haley saw a shiny sports car pull up, driven by Matthew Graham. He honked, and Whitney waved to him and got into the car. So Whitney was hooking up with Matthew Graham now? What next, Coco and Spencer back together?

Well, yes. Walking past Bubbies Bistro that evening, Haley saw Coco at a table in the window—with Spencer. He was spooning chocolate mousse into her mouth. *So,* Haley figured, *the big freeze must be over—and the big diet too.* But why hadn't she gotten the memo?

"What exactly is going on?" Haley asked Coco at school the next day. "Everybody seems to have given up on Operation Dump 'Em except for me."

"We haven't given up," Coco said. "We just revised the doctrine."

"So that it allows hugging, kissing and feeding each other desserts?"

"Basically," Coco said. "Look, it was getting old, okay? Lighten up."

Haley felt betrayed. She had gone along with Coco's doctrine wholeheartedly, following her schemes to the letter. And now it was all over, just like that? Somehow it didn't seem right. The boys had still done them wrong. As far as Haley could tell, they'd barely paid any price for their misdeeds at all. The girls had given in too easily.

Then, after school that day, Reese approached her and asked to talk.

"I'm tired of the silence between us," he said. "I miss having you to talk to. I miss having you on my side, or in the stands at a game cheering me on."

"I'm sorry I hurt you," she said. "But you hurt me first. Do you know how it felt to open up those photos of you?"

"I can only imagine," Reese said. "But I didn't mean to—I swear. Haley, I'd like to get back together with you. I'd like to explain what happened if I can."

Haley's tongue felt paralyzed. She didn't know what to say. She was glad to hear that Reese still liked her. But could all the pain that had passed between them be wiped away so easily? The other girls seemed to have forgotten all about their heartache. But Haley wasn't so sure she could forget about hers.

• • •

What should Haley do? Here is Reese on his knees before her, begging to get back together. If he had done that two months earlier, she might have given in right away.

The other girls seem to have dropped their revenge plots without a second thought. To be honest, Haley's a little disappointed in them. How spineless could they be? More importantly, she's not sure that's the right thing to do. What if she takes Reese back and he turns around and hurts her again? She doesn't think she could survive a second betrayal.

On the other hand . . . it's Reese. What if he's the one she was meant to be with? What if there's a good explanation for his antics in Nevis? How can she turn him down? After all, he's taking a big risk right now too, laying it all out there and asking Haley to take him back. He knows she could send him packing, even if all her girlfriends already gave in and are back to canoodling with their guys.

If you think Haley is still in love with Reese but shouldn't listen to her heart because it might be rebroken, turn to page 310, LONELY ONE. If you think Haley should give Reese another chance, set her PRIORITIES STRAIGHT on page 306.

PRIORITIES STRAIGHT

A good guy usually deserves a second chance.

Haley crossed her arms and looked Reese straight in the eye. "I'm still listening," she said. "Tell me more. What exactly went on down there?"

"It was awful," Reese said. They sat leaning against the lockers in the hallway, settling in for a long talk. "Spencer promised the trip was going to be quiet and sober, just the guys swimming and playing volleyball and relaxing away from any temptations. And I believed him, because his mother set the whole thing up, and I knew how much she wanted him to stay out of trouble before her big inauguration."

Haley laughed. "That's a losing proposition. Trouble just seems to follow Spencer, no matter where he goes."

"Yeah, her plan couldn't have backfired more, could it?" Reese was laughing too. "Those pictures are plastered all over the Internet."

"Speaking of plastered," Haley said. "What were you guys on? You looked wasted in a lot of those shots."

"That was the problem. We get to the resort and there are all these models there for a photo shoot, and Spencer basically says, 'Screw quiet and sober, let's party!' The other guys were into it but I really wasn't. I talked to a few of those girls and they were vaporheads. All they wanted to know was who had the blow. So I sat by myself on the beach while the other guys whooped it up. Finally one of the girls brought me some papaya juice. That's what she told me it was, anyway. It turned out Spencer had spiked it."

"Figures," Haley said.

"Yeah, I should have known. I'm not used to drinking, so I got sloshed pretty quickly. But believe me, I'm not planning on drinking again—it turned me into such a jackass. I hated the way I was acting, but it was like I was outside my body watching someone who looked just like me be a jerk. The next morning when I woke up, I felt so disgusted and ashamed. I don't believe in treating women like strippers. And I was terrified that you'd find out what happened and misunderstand. And then I found out the pictures were online and all over Hillsdale."

"Not to mention on my cell phone, before I'd even gotten a Happy New Year message from you." Haley appreciated Reese telling her the details, and she believed him. Still, if he got drunk and acted like a fool once, he could do it again, no matter what he said.

"I just didn't know what to say to you, Haley." Reese looked mortified. "You mean so much to me, and I felt like an animal for disrespecting you. I couldn't find the right words to apologize. And then, when I saw you at school and you wouldn't speak to me, well, I just thought I'd blown my only chance."

Haley thought long and hard about Reese. "I'm willing to give you another shot," she told him finally. "As a friend. Just for a while. If things seem to be going well, maybe we can work our way back toward what we had before. But I'm warning you, we're a long way from that."

"That's fair." Reese laid his hand on top of hers. A gesture of friendship, she supposed, but it felt like more. "That's all I can ask for."

She smiled at him and he gazed back at her. She was glad to be friends with him again. She could see in his face what a good person he was. And soon she was drowning in those warm blue eyes.

I'm a goner, she thought. *We'll be back together in no time.*

But suddenly that didn't seem like such a bad thing.

THE END

LONELY ONE

Being rigid only makes a person easier to snap in two.

"Haley, listen to me," Reese pleaded as Haley eyed him skeptically. "Spencer spiked my drink on that island. I didn't know what I was doing. It wasn't my fault, at least not entirely."

But Haley couldn't get those pictures out of her mind: the shots of Reese with his hands all over some bikini-clad model, umbrellas everywhere, even in the drinks. . . . Which was the real Reese? The lecherous, drunken two-timer, or the earnest boy pleading his case in front of her right now?

Haley felt she had no way of knowing, that she'd never really know for certain what was going on in Reese's mind—or how he really felt about her. Sure, now that he was back in Hillsdale and there were no bathing suit models around to distract him, he wanted to get back with Haley. But what about the next time temptation reared its head? Or the next time his pal Spencer spiked his drink? Would Reese be strong, or would he succumb?

"Haley? I've got to know your answer," Reese said. "I can't stand another minute in limbo like this. Do you believe me or not?"

"Nice try," Haley said. "But I have no interest in wasting my time with a two-timing cheat. The pictures don't lie, Reese. Only boys do. Sorry."

She felt good as she strode away; she felt strong. She'd stuck to her principles. She'd stuck with the plan.

Coco's plan.

The trouble was, Coco wasn't even sticking to it anymore. And neither was Cecily, Sasha or Whitney.

Everywhere Haley went that week she saw one of them nuzzling with their now-rehabilitated exes. There were Sasha and Johnny, making out by their lockers. There were Coco and Spencer, walking hand in hand through the halls. There were Cecily and Drew, cuddling in the cafeteria. And there were Whitney and Matt Graham, newly hooked up and huddled together near his car, Matt's eyes glued to Whitney's cleavage.

Spring was in the air, and romance was blossoming for everyone except Haley. She watched Reese from a distance all week, wishing she had someone to hold hands with too.

Maybe I was too rough on him, she thought. *Maybe I made a mistake, blowing him off that way. After all, he did apologize, and Spencer may really have been the one who got him drunk. It does sound like something Spencer would do. . . .*

She thought of tossing away her dignity and begging Reese to take her back. Whenever she ran into him at school or in the neighborhood, she found herself staring at him longingly. But he didn't return the stare. He only turned his back on her and walked away.

The message was clear: he was over her now. There was no point in trying to get him back, Haley realized. In her stubbornness in refusing to forgive him, she'd lost Reese for good.

THE END